LOVE POTION DARCY'S MINE

A PRIDE AND PREJUDICE VARIATION

VIOLET KING

PEMBERLEY PLAYGROUND PRESS

Can a love born in scandal and spellcraft lead to true happiness?

When Caroline Bingley purchases a love potion to win Mr. Darcy's heart, things go horribly awry, leading to a scandalous kiss between Elizabeth and Mr. Darcy! Compromised and confused, Elizabeth and Mr. Darcy join forces to discover the source of their sudden passion. But a conniving Caroline will not let one failure keep her from becoming the Mistress of Pemberley. And when Lady Catherine and Mr. Wickham enter the fray, Elizabeth and Mr. Darcy's fragile trust is pushed to the breaking point. Can a love born in scandal and spellcraft lead to true happiness?

Let the magic of Mr. Darcy sweep you away in this laugh out loud Pride and Prejudice variation of 50,000 words. Includes sweet romance, saucy humor, and a HEA guaranteed.

Miss Caroline Bingley picked her way by moonlight from her carriage along the narrow, winding path where her lady's maid, Margaret, had promised the peddler's wagon would be waiting. An icy breeze tore through the boughs of the ancient trees on either side. Miss Bingley clutched her shawl ever more tightly to her shoulders. The unfortunate lady silently cursed her maid for sending her on such a foolish errand on so chill an autumn night. If this turned out to be nothing but one of Margaret's absurd jests, Caroline would see the foolish girl without a character reference by morn.

The path made an abrupt turn, and ten paces ahead,

the moon cast an eerie glow over a dilapidated wagon. Caroline clutched the pouch of coins, her knuckles turning white, as she glimpsed a faint light gleaming through the wagon's curtains.

So Margaret was correct. The mysterious peddler who sold the key to true love was here.

An owl hooted softly in the distance, sending a shiver down Caroline's spine, but she steeled her nerves. She had not come this far to back out now. By God, love was the one thing her fortune could not buy, but she was determined to have it.

Summoning her courage, Caroline rapped sharply on the worn wooden door. "Mr. Alistair Beaumont?"

The door creaked open to reveal one of the most peculiar figures Miss Bingley had ever beheld. Mr. Beaumont's clothes hung from his wiry frame as though hastily they had been draped over a scarecrow. His dark, deep-set eyes seemed to hold both secrets and a touch of mockery. Surely, Caroline thought, this could not be the one who held the key to Mr. Darcy's heart.

The bizarre gentleman peered at Caroline with an

inscrutable expression. "Ah Miss Bingley, I was expecting you," he drawled in a mocking tone.

How had he known she was coming? Caroline stifled a gasp. Her courage wavered but a moment before her desire for Mr. Darcy's hand steeled her nerves once more.

"Were you?" she asked, screwing her courage to the sticking place.

"Indeed," he replied, stepping aside and beckoning her into the dimly lit wagon. "Please, do come in."

As she stepped inside, Caroline's gaze was immediately drawn to the multitude of trinkets and bottles lining the shelves. She could not help but stare at the sight of something that appeared to be constructed from the bones of some unfortunate rodent. Creepy, and intentionally so. Surely, she mused, this man was nothing more than a charlatan. And yet...

Amidst the clutter, her eyes settled on a small vial labeled 'elixir amoris'. Could this be it? Would potion bind her beloved Mr. Darcy to her?

Mr. Beaumont followed her gaze, a knowing smile

playing at the corners of his crooked mouth. "Ah, I see you've found our most popular item."

Caroline eyed him skeptically, her heart pounding despite herself. "And does it truly work?"

Mr. Beaumont shrugged, leaning against the worn wooden counter. "That depends entirely on your definition of 'work,' my dear."

Caroline scoffed. "Well, I expect it to make a gentleman fall madly in love with me, of course."

"Ah," the peddler nodded sagely, "but love is such a fickle thing, is it not? Can one truly bottle and sell it like some common tonic?"

Caroline frowned, her patience wearing thin. "You do not give me the confidence I require in this transaction, Mr. Beaumont."

The peddler grinned, revealing a row of crooked teeth. "My apologies, Miss Bingley. Perhaps I can offer you a different potion instead? I have one that's said to cure warts, and another that guarantees a fortnight of fair weather!"

Caroline pursed her lips, irritation threatening to

overshadow her desperation. "I want the love potion, Mr. Beaumont, and I will pay handsomely for it."

Mr. Beaumont's grin widened, his eyes sparkling with mischief. "Very well. But remember, Miss Bingley—love cannot be bought or forced. Sometimes, it must simply be... allowed."

Caroline rolled her eyes, reluctantly handing over the pouch of coins. "Spare me the cryptic nonsense, peddler. Just give me the potion."

With a dramatic flourish, Mr. Beaumont placed the vial into her outstretched hand. As Caroline Bingley walked away from the peddler's wagon, clutching the elixir she hoped would win her Mr. Darcy's heart forever, she could have sworn she heard the faintest sound of laughter in the wind.

CHAPTER ONE

The Netherfield ball was in full swing. A sea of guests in colorful gowns and tailored coats swirled with laughter as they stepped and twirled on the dance floor. The ballroom's grandeur surpassed Elizabeth's expectations, and certainly those of her mother, who had pointed and gasped at everything from the marble floors to the exquisite glassware and the glittering chandeliers. Elizabeth, standing at the edge of the dance floor, also found herself swept up in the excitement as ladies in their elegant gowns and gentlemen in dashing suits mingled, laughter and gossip filling the air.

"Jane, my dear," Elizabeth teased, her eyes scanning the room, "Be cautious lest Mr. Collins set his sights on you next. He has all the virtues of an overly verbose peacock, twirling about!"

"Lizzy!" replied Jane, attempting to suppress a giggle and failing. "I am sure any lady would be flattered if it were not so difficult to tell whether he is dancing or merely attempting to avoid collisions with the other gentlemen."

"Collisions! Such collisions indeed!" exclaimed Mrs. Bennet, joining their conversation with her usual flourish. "Observe, my dears, how Mr. Bingley's gaze never strays from our sweet Jane!"

"Mother," protested Jane, brushing at an invisible speck of dust on her gown.

"Oh, do not fret, my dear," Mrs. Bennet assured her eldest daughter, patting her hand. "I am certain Mr. Bingley will make you an offer before the night is through!"

Jane's cheeks went bright red, and she averted her gaze, but Elizabeth noticed a small smile playing at the corners of her sister's lips.

"And what of you, Lizzy?" asked Mrs. Bennet. "There

is no doubt your esteemed cousin, Mr. Collins, has his eye on you."

Elizabeth was also certain that was the case and had done all in her power to avoid her cousin's attentions. Even so, Mr. Collins had laid claim to two dances. The only thing preventing the rumors of an incipient proposal was their familial relationship as cousins and that Mr. Collins' manners were frankly ridiculous.

"And there is our dear host now!" Mrs. Bennet proclaimed loudly enough to draw the attention of several nearby guests. Her expression soured. "And with him, of course, Mr. Darcy."

Elizabeth followed her mother's gaze to where Charles Bingley was standing with his sister, Miss Caroline Bingley, and Mr. Darcy. The latter was a tall man with dark hair and brooding eyes, his handsome features marred by a perpetual look of scorn.

"I do not know why Mr. Bingley insists on associating with such an ill-mannered man," huffed Mrs. Bennet. "Mr. Darcy looks down upon us all as if we are mere commoners!"

"Mama!" Jane said, her tone low and kind. "A certain

reserve does not always speak of disdain. Perhaps Mr. Darcy is merely shy."

"Shy?" scoffed Mrs. Bennet. "After the insult he gave your sister! And I have never seen him speak more than two words to anyone at these balls! He is simply too proud to mingle with the rest of us."

Elizabeth hated to agree with her mother, but she could not deny the truth in her words. Mr. Darcy had been nothing but rude and arrogant since his arrival in Hertfordshire, and she grew more irritated by his presence with each passing day. And yet, there was something about him that intrigued her.

After another minute, as the musicians began again to tune their instruments, to Mrs. Bennet's audible delight, Mr. Bingley stepped away from his sister and friend.

"He means to ask for a dance," Mrs. Bennet said. "And he means to ask Jane's hand!"

"Mama!" Jane hissed, but again, Elizabeth saw the hope in her sister's eyes.

Mr. Bingley approached with a warm smile and a

polite bow. "Good evening, ladies," he said cheerfully.

"Oh, Mr. Bingley," Mrs. Bennet gushed, "what a wonderful ball this is! I have never seen such splendor!" She continued with increasing embellishment, "And the music is so lovely! And the refreshments! I declare it is the finest ball I have ever attended!"

"You are too kind, madam," replied Mr. Bingley, his eyes sparkling with amusement. "And Miss Bennet? I hope everything has been to your comfort."

Jane gave Mr. Bingley a brief nod, her cheeks pinking slightly as her fingers fluttered over her gown. It was a subtle display, and one Elizabeth feared might be too subtle. She wished Jane would be more forthright about her affections for Mr. Bingley.

Mrs. Bennet, however, was not so reserved. "Oh, yes, my dear Jane has been most comfortable, and I am sure she is looking forward to dancing with you."

While Jane and Mr. Bingley made pleasantries, and Mrs. Bennet interjected with occasional unpleasantries, Elizabeth's gaze drifted to Mr. Darcy and Miss Bingley, who seemed engaged in an animated conversation. Miss Bingley's expression was one of smug satisfaction as she spoke to the brooding Mr. Darcy, whose countenance remained inscrutable.

If Elizabeth had to hazard a guess, she would say Mr. Darcy seemed bored, and perhaps a bit irritated, though Elizabeth doubted she could discern annoyance from his usual countenance. Then he turned his gaze to her, and a jolt of electricity shot through her body as their eyes locked. His dark eyes widened, and for a moment, she thought she saw something akin to admiration in his expression. But just as quickly as it appeared, it was gone. His features hardened once more, and he turned away, giving Miss Bingley his full attention.

Elizabeth felt a strange mixture of disappointment and relief. She did not want to admit it, but there was something about Mr. Darcy that intrigued her, despite his arrogant demeanor.

As the musicians finished tuning their instruments, Mr. Bingley turned to Jane with a hopeful smile. "Miss Bennet, would you do me the honor of this dance?"

Jane nodded demurely, and Elizabeth watched as

Jane took Mr. Bingley's arm and they started together towards the dance floor.

Mrs. Bennet looked on with pride, beaming at her daughters. "Oh, Lizzy! Do you see? I knew Mr. Bingley would ask for Jane's hand in a dance!"

"Yes, Mama," said Elizabeth, trying to keep the exasperation from her voice.

Mr. Collins approached with an exaggerated bow. "Cousin Elizabeth," he said in a loud voice that was certain to draw attention. "I believe it is time for our dance."

"Indeed," Elizabeth said, swallowing a sigh.

Mr. Collins was light on his feet, embellishing each movement of body and conversation. His greatest enthusiasm came as he spoke at length about the superiority of his patroness. "Lady Catherine de Bourgh says that dancing is an excellent way to improve one's posture," he declared as they stepped in time to the music.

"I am sure she is right, Mr. Collins," Elizabeth said dryly.

"And Lady Catherine de Bourgh says that proper

dancing posture will ensure a long life and good health!" Mr. Collins continued, oblivious to Elizabeth's sarcasm. "Why, Lady Catherine's posture is so perfect, her housekeeper proclaims the lady has hardly suffered from a day's illness since she was born!"

"Indeed," Elizabeth returned.

"It is a pity you do not have such a fine patroness as Lady Catherine de Bourgh," Mr. Collins continued. "I am sure she could advise you on how best to care for your own posture." He blinked, and perhaps realizing his error, added, "That is, I am sure you are doing the very best you can. Your posture is not bad at all, truly, but in all ways, we must endeavor to improve."

Elizabeth bit her tongue, trying not to laugh at Mr. Collins's clumsy attempts at flattery. "Thank you, Mr. Collins," she said with mock sincerity.

"You are most welcome. It is to your credit that you recognize the value of such advice, Miss Elizabeth..."

Elizabeth endured Mr. Collins' endless chatter, doing her best to feign interest, but her thoughts kept drifting back to Mr. Darcy and his strange expression. Surely he had no tender feelings towards her, a lady he had proclaimed "not handsome enough to dance with" mere weeks ago. One whose accomplishments were not of the depth or breadth to meet his exacting standards.

Between a step, spin, and turn, Elizabeth again glimpsed Mr. Darcy. He, Miss Bingley, and Mrs. Hurst stood at the edge of the dance floor. Both ladies slowly waved ostrich feather fans over their faces and neck as Mr. Hurst approached, carrying four drinks on a small tray.

Miss Bingley stepped away from the group and, snapping her fan closed, took two of the drinks with an expansive display of concern. Elizabeth turned and spun again, returning to her place in time to see Miss Bingley stumble, her fingers fluttering over the mouth of the glass.

Odd. Elizabeth frowned. It almost appeared Miss Bingley had dropped something into one of the pair of drinks. But why?

Mr. Collins said, "Miss Elizabeth? Is something amiss?"

Elizabeth blinked. "No, I am well."

"I trust you know I meant no insult earlier. I am certain Lady Catherine would be most impressed with your dancing abilities. You are adept for one who does not practice daily."

Elizabeth smiled tightly, tempering her response to a simple, "Indeed."

Mr. Collins continued in a similar vein, but Elizabeth could not help but watch Miss Bingley as she returned to her companions. She handed a glass to Mr. Darcy, who took it with a polite nod.

Perhaps Miss Bingley had dosed Mr. Darcy's drink with spirits? Gin? It seemed unlikely. More likely, anything Elizabeth had seen was a trick of movement and candlelight.

Finally, the song ended, and Elizabeth curtsied to Mr. Collins.

"As cousins, it is not improper for us to have a third dance," Mr. Collins suggested. "Dancing itself is—"

As Elizabeth opened her mouth to claim overexertion and an immediate need to visit the ladies' parlor to relieve herself, she saw Mr. Darcy striding towards them both.

"I believe that's Mr. Darcy," Elizabeth commented, inclining her chin towards the esteemed Lady Catherine's also esteemed nephew.

"Mr. Darcy?" Mr. Collins, as expected, turned immediately, dropping into an overly formal and wholly unnecessary bow.

Elizabeth, more out of habit than necessity, fell into a curtsy. A wholly unnecessary curtsy. Her cousin's manners were catching. Elizabeth wrinkled her nose at the thought. "I assume you gentlemen have business," she said.

But to Elizabeth's surprise, Mr. Darcy gave Mr. Collins no sign of acknowledgement at all. Instead, his gaze focused on her. "Miss Elizabeth," he said, his deep voice sending a shiver of mingled nerves and delight through her. "I believe you promised me this dance."

Elizabeth stared at him in confusion, her heart pounding. "Did I?"

She knew she ought to protest as she had done no

such thing, but she found herself strangely unable to form the words.

"Indeed," said Mr. Darcy, offering her his arm with a look of intense determination. "I insist."

Elizabeth hesitated for a moment before taking Mr. Darcy's arm and allowing him to lead her back onto the dance floor.

CHAPTER TWO

A heat, focus, and determination rose in Darcy as he led Miss Elizabeth to take their place on the dance floor. There was a rightness to the feel of her hand on the crook of his arm, and an awareness that seemed to be growing between them. He could not explain it, nor did he wish to resist it.

Miss Elizabeth had fascinated him since she had arrived at Netherfield, her face flushed and gown in disarray, intending to care for her sister. While sisterly devotion was surely a virtue, Darcy recognized hiking miles through the countryside was not proper behavior for a lady. And yet... there was something in that rebellion that made him want to learn more about her.

"Mr. Darcy," Miss Elizabeth said, a hint of amusement in her voice as they took their place in the line of dancers.

His gaze drifted to her lips, and for a moment, he wondered what it would be like to kiss them.

"I am afraid I do not recall promising you a dance," Miss Elizabeth continued, her tone light and teasing.

"Forgive me for my forwardness, but you did not seem enamored with your cousin's dancing abilities."

Miss Elizabeth laughed, a bright, musical sound that sent a wave of warmth through Darcy's chest. "Perhaps not," she replied. "But I had not thought you would be so willing to risk the tedium of dancing with a lady of so few accomplishments."

Darcy smiled, his gaze never leaving hers. "No gentleman would dare accuse you of tedium."

"Perhaps I misheard. Did you intend that as a compliment, Mr. Darcy?"

"You did not mishear."

Miss Elizabeth raised an eyebrow, her eyes sparkling

with amusement. "I see," she said, quirking an eyebrow. "So you have finally come to recognize my many virtues?"

Darcy felt an unexpected rush of desire at her words. The power of it frightened and confused him, and he was grateful in that moment that the music forced them to step away from each other to turn, step, and briefly change partners. He could hardly focus on the next lady, Miss Charlotte Lucas. Her expression was serious, her figure rather square, and her gown a shade of blue that did her complexion no favors. Then the dance directed him again, placing him face to face with Charles's sister, Miss Bingley.

"Mr. Darcy," she said, her eyes wide and expectant. She swept her tongue over her lower lip. "I had hoped we might share a second dance."

Darcy, distracted by his growing and frightening need to return to Miss Elizabeth, to touch her, to feel her hands on his skin, murmured something noncommittal.

Miss Bingley's expression shuttered, and, as the dance separated them again, Darcy felt a wave of guilt wash over him. He knew he had been rude, but he could not bring himself to care. His thoughts were consumed with Miss Elizabeth and the strange desire growing inside him.

When they returned to their place in the line, Darcy could not resist the urge to draw closer to Miss Elizabeth. "Miss Elizabeth," he said a little breathlessly.

Miss Elizabeth's eyes widened, and her lips trembled as he took her hands.

"You are an excellent dancer," Darcy said. Though the hall was crowded and sweat trickled along the nape of his neck, the heat radiating between them seemed to create its own intimate bubble. Miss Elizabeth smelled of lavender and fresh air, and Darcy wanted nothing more than to press his lips against hers.

Miss Elizabeth's cheeks were flushed, though whether in response to his compliment or the exertion of the dance, he didn't know. She dipped her chin in a shallow nod. "Thank you, Mr. Darcy." Her beautiful, full lips quirked as she added, "While I cannot practice daily, I hope my posture is to your satisfaction."

"Your posture?" What possible care could he have for her posture? An image of pushing her back against a wall and pressing his mouth to hers, feeling her go rigid and then soft in his arms flashed through Darcy's mind, sending a wave of desire through him that nearly caused him to stumble.

Elizabeth stepped forward, steadying him, and their faces came close enough he felt her breath on his cheek. "Yes," she said, her tone teasing but seductive. "Lady Catherine de Bourgh says proper posture—"

Something in Darcy broke, that part of himself that knew himself bound by proper behavior, and he slipped a hand behind her head as he pressed his lips to hers. It was a gentle touch, barely a brush of lips on lips.

Miss Elizabeth went stiff in surprise. "Mr. Da—" She swallowed, her tongue sweeping between her lips as though tasting something sweet. Perhaps the remnants of the too-sweet drink Miss Bingley had insisted he finish himself before beginning this next dance.

"My apologies," Darcy managed, though that brief

meeting of lips had done nothing to curb his need for her.

Miss Elizabeth pressed her lips together, and Darcy feared she might slap him. If not with her hand, with her words. Then she leaned in again, her pupils widening to crowd out the brown of her irises, as she lifted her chin and pressed her lips against his. Darcy's heart pounded so loudly in his chest he feared everyone might hear it. His desire roared through him, building until he could no longer resist the urge to wrap an arm around her waist and pull her closer, deepening the kiss.

She melted against him, her lips parting. She let out a soft moan as he tangled his fingers in her curls, wanting nothing more than to draw her even closer, to feel the warmth of her body against his—

"Mr. Darcy!"

Was that Mr. Collins, his aunt's odious vicar and sycophant? Darcy ignored him, much preferring the heat and softness of Miss Elizabeth's mouth.

"Mr. Darcy!" Mr. Collins said again, louder this time. The music screeched to a halt as sounds of shock and scandal rose from the guests.

Miss Elizabeth pulled away from Darcy's embrace, her eyes wide with shock and confusion. "I—" she began, but before she could say anything else, Mr. Collins stepped between them, his face red with anger and indignation.

"Mr. Darcy," he shouted, his voice shaking with rage. "I must insist that you unhand my cousin at once!"

The room seemed to spin around Darcy as he struggled to regain his composure. Finally, when he could muster words to speak again, he said, "Miss Elizabeth and I are engaged to wed."

Miss Elizabeth's mouth fell open, her fingers fluttering over her lips in obvious shock as the crowd gasped in disbelief.

"Surely not!" Miss Bingley shouted. "You've spoken nothing of this, Mr. Darcy. You have no obligation to this—! This fortune hunter who—!"

"Caroline!" Bingley snapped, grabbing his sister's forearm and squeezing it to silence his sister's increasing vitriol. "If Darcy says he is engaged, then I must insist we respect his honor. And the honor of our guests."

Bless Bingley's loyalty. The man's father might have been closer to trade than was acceptable for a gentleman of Darcy's status, but he had the virtue of living without pretense. When Bingley gave his friendship, it was true.

Mr. Collins sputtered, "But Mr. Darcy! You cannot mean to marry my cousin! She is not at all suitable for you. Lady Catherine would never approve!"

Ignoring Mr. Collins, Darcy took Miss Elizabeth's hand. He did not understand what madness had overcome him. Whatever had possessed him to press himself so forcefully upon Miss Elizabeth, a lady he barely knew, on the dance floor of his friend's ball-room, he knew that if he did not insist on this engagement, he would have irrevocably ruined Miss Elizabeth's reputation. He could not, in honor, inflict such harm on an innocent.

"We are, as I said, engaged to wed. The banns will be read on Sunday." Darcy would make certain of that. If he had not made such a display of himself, he would have gone to his uncle, the Earl, and asked him to petition the bishop of Canterbury for a Special License. Unfortunately, departing so suddenly, possibly for a week, would be almost as damaging to Miss Elizabeth's reputation as not marrying her at all.

Mrs. Bennet elbowed her way through the crowd, her face ruddy and eyes bright with barely repressed excitement. "Engaged to wed our Lizzy!" she exclaimed, clapping her hands together in glee. "Oh! What joy! What joy!" She turned to Miss Elizabeth, who still seemed too stunned to speak. "Lizzy! My dear girl! How could you keep such a secret from your own mother? Oh! But I am sure you were waiting for the right moment to make your announcement. And this was, certainly, a most dramatic moment! Most dramatic!"

Miss Elizabeth, seeming for once lost for words, simply nodded.

CHAPTER THREE

After accepting, or, more accurately, being thrown like a dinghy through rushing rapids and over the falls into Mr. Darcy's proposal, Elizabeth's departure from Netherfield was a blur.

At least Mrs. Bennet was pleased. She went on for the entire carriage ride home with exclamations of, "Oh! What joy! What joy! Our Lizzy engaged to Mr. Darcy!" and "Oh, what a fine wedding it will be! And what a wedding breakfast! We must insist on Netherfield! I wonder, Mr. Collins, will Mr. Darcy persuade his aunt, Lady Catherine de Bourgh, to attend?"

Mr. Collins sat at Elizabeth's right and across from Mrs. Bennet as her mother had insisted on the journey to Netherfield, his ruddy face a mix of colicky and sour. "I cannot speak for Lady Catherine de Bourgh," he said, "but I am sure she would not wish to attend such a hasty wedding."

"Hasty!" exclaimed Mrs. Bennet, her eyes wide with shock and offense. "Mr. Collins!"

Lydia, seated at her mother's left, muttered, "I suppose this is one way to ensure you are the first of your sisters wed."

"You could learn something from your sister." Mrs. Bennet turned towards Lydia, her tone sharp. "If you were more like Lizzy—"

A worm of mirth squirmed in Elizabeth's chest at her mother's words. She'd have thought herself dead and buried before her mother declared Elizabeth superior to her darling Lydia. Let alone to have Mrs. Bennet insist Lydia act more like Elizabeth! Perhaps she was still in her bed at Longbourn dreaming. Or perhaps she lay abed, delirious from some plague. That was as likely as the events of this evening: Mr. Darcy's kiss. Elizabeth's response. And Mrs. Bennet's approbation.

"Mama," Jane interjected, her tone soft but firm. She sat on Elizabeth's opposite side. "I am sure Mr. Collins did not intend any insult to Elizabeth or Mr. Darcy."

"I also believe Mr. Darcy and Lady Catherine's esteemed daughter, Miss Anne de Bourgh, have an understanding," Mr. Collins added with no attempt at apology, his tone instead smug.

Elizabeth's skin felt cold. She knew little of Mr. Darcy's family beyond that which she had gleaned from gossip and Mr. Collins' incessant praise of Lady Catherine. But if he was engaged to another...

No.

Mr. Darcy would not have been so rakish as to insist on a proposal if he was promised to another. Then again, how much did she know about Mr. Darcy? She would never have suspected him capable of genuine passion. Certainly not for Elizabeth. He had shown little interest in her prior to the ball, where he had kissed her with the fervor of a man possessed by the devil himself.

What troubled her more was how fervently she had

31

kissed him back. That brief touch, the sweet, effervescent taste of his lips, had ignited something within her. Something primal and all-encompassing. Elizabeth shook her head, ignoring her mother's protest that Mr. Darcy could not have been so dishonorable as to declare an engagement without the intent to follow through.

The carriage came to a halt before Longbourn, and Elizabeth followed her mother and younger sisters inside, her head still spinning.

Jane, walking beside Elizabeth, took her hand. "Lizzy, how long have you and Mr. Darcy...?" She sounded hurt, and Elizabeth realized Jane thought Elizabeth had somehow been engaging in a secret courtship. A conclusion that sadly made more sense than the truth.

Elizabeth shook her head. "I kept nothing from you. I promise." She squeezed her sister's hand, hoping to send the sincerity of her words through their touch.

As they passed through the entranceway, Mrs. Bennet shouted with enough volume to shake the walls, "Mr. Bennet! Oh! We are home! Mr. Bennet!

And our Lizzy, how clever she is, has brought us the most delightful news!"

Elizabeth's father appeared in the doorway of his study, his expression bemused. "Lizzy? The ball is over already?"

"Our Lizzy is engaged! To Mr. Darcy! She will be mistress of the Pemberley estate in Derbyshire!" Mrs. Bennet exclaimed before Elizabeth could speak a word. "And the banns will be read on Sunday!"

Mr. Bennet's eyes widened, his expression a mask of bewilderment. "Mr... who?"

"Mr. Fitzwilliam Darcy," Mrs. Bennet waved a hand dismissively, as if Mr. Bennet had implied Mr. Darcy was not a flesh and blood gentleman and some figment of her imagination. "He is worth ten thousand a year! And he is Lady Catherine de Bourgh's nephew. Mr. Collins, has spoken extensively of her virtues. Mr. Collins?" She looked around, only then noting the vicar's absence.

Elizabeth, who had also forgotten about her cousin after leaving the carriage, rubbed her hand over her forehead to relieve some of the growing pressure of what she suspected was an impending megrim.

"We are all well aware of Lady Catherine de Bourgh," Mr. Bennet agreed. "That is beside the point, my dear Mrs. Bennet. What is this of an engagement? I am sure I would remember if my daughter was engaged to a Mr. Fitzwilliam Darcy." Mr. Bennet's gaze shifted to Elizabeth. "Lizzy, is this true? Surely, this is an oddly timed jest."

Elizabeth swallowed hard, trying to keep her composure. "It is not jest, Papa."

Mr. Bennet frowned, his brow furrowing as he studied Elizabeth's face. "I see," he said slowly, clearly unconvinced. "The same Mr. Darcy who was so rude to you at the most recent Meryton assembly, yes? And when did you become engaged to Mr. Darcy?"

Elizabeth scraped her teeth over her lower lip, shifting on her feet as she had as a child when she had snuck into her father's study to steal sweets from his desk. She had never been able to lie to him then, and it was no easier now. "Tonight."

Mr. Bennet blinked. "I beg your pardon?"

Lydia, who had been rocking back and forth on her

feet, her expression one of barely suppressed glee, blurted out, "He kissed her in front of everyone! On the dance floor! It was a terrible scandal! They had no choice but to claim an engagement."

"Lydia!" Mrs. Bennet snapped. "You will not speak of your sister in such a tone!"

Elizabeth's sister Mary, who had, like Kitty, remained silent until this moment, cut in, "Mama is correct, Lydia. As it says in the book of Common Prayers: 'Let your light so shine before men that they may see your good works and glorify your father which is in heaven.'" She paused, her brow furrowing as she added, "Though I believe Elizabeth's actions, kissing Mr. Darcy with such vigor in full view of the entire ballroom, are not precisely what the Lord intended when he spoke those words."

Mr. Bennet's bushy gray eyebrows shot straight up.

Elizabeth pressed her lips together in frustration. She did not want to be reminded that her actions were not what a proper young lady ought to do. She knew that. Or she ought to have. What possessed her to return Mr. Darcy's kiss? Yes, Mr.

Darcy was handsome, but he had treated her until that moment with profound disregard. What had possessed the gentleman to insist upon a dance, let alone...?

Her lips, her whole body, tingled with the memory of their kiss. The passion in that brief touch had rivaled any proclamation of love in verse or amatory tale. And it terrified her.

"Elizabeth," Mr. Bennet said, and the use of her full name and not 'Lizzy" only increased Elizabeth's sense of guilt and shame. "If we could have a word in private." He beckoned her into his study.

"Yes, Papa," Elizabeth said softly, unable to meet her father's gaze as she followed him inside, the door falling shut behind them.

Elizabeth felt as though she were a child again, about to be scolded for some transgression. Worse, she felt she deserved the scolding. What had happened to send her so far from her head that she threw propriety and good sense to the wind to kiss Mr. Darcy, of all people, in full public display at Mr. Bingley's ball? The ball which should have been about seeing to her beloved sister Jane's future happiness.

Mr. Bennet gestured for her to take a seat in one of the chairs before his desk, and Elizabeth obliged him, sinking into the worn leather with a sigh.

"Now," Mr. Bennet said, taking his own seat behind the desk. "Of all my children, I've always felt you and I had the most similar temperament." An expression of weariness settled over Mr. Bennet's features. "So I suppose it should not surprise me that your lapses in judgment so closely resemble mine. Had I been ruled more by my head than my loins..." he sighed, his gaze drifting to the bookshelves that lined the walls. "Well, it does not matter now."

"Papa!" Elizabeth choked out. She had known her parents' marriage was not, at its core, a happy one. They did not have loud, angry rows as sometimes Charlotte's parents did, but sometimes Elizabeth wondered if explosions might have been preferable to her father's subtle mockery and removal to his study, and her mother's insistence that all would be solved if only she could give him a son. Or now, if only she could find each of her daughters a magnificent match.

Despite her mother's aggressive cheer and her father's mix of self-imposed isolation and ill-timed jests, Elizabeth knew they cared for each other. Even if their love was marred by neither understanding the other's true nature until after they spoke their vows.

And Elizabeth, who had sworn in her heart only to marry for love, had made an even more spurious match than her parents. One based entirely on a moment of lust. The memory of that kiss pulsed through her, and she hated how much she wanted again to taste Mr. Darcy's lips, to feel his arms around her.

She was a fool. And no matter how much her mother crowed about Mr. Darcy's ten thousand a year, no amount of riches could buy Elizabeth back the dream of love she had so callously set aside.

Mr. Bennet sighed heavily, rubbing his hand over his forehead. "So how long were the two of you courting in secret, then?"

"We were not."

Mr. Bennet barked a laugh. "I find it highly unlikely a gentleman of Mr. Fitzwilliam Darcy's means would make such an offer without some prior attachment between you."

Elizabeth found it unlikely that a gentleman of any kind would have taken such an improper step as to kiss her without having had some prior attachment, let alone to do so on a crowded ballroom dancefloor. "It was sudden," Elizabeth explained. "At first, when our lips touched, I felt nothing but shock. And then..." Elizabeth remembered the hint of sweetness from his kiss, the tingling through her lips that seemed to catch fire through her whole body, turning what had been a slight sense of interest into a wildfire of curiosity and desire.

Mr. Bennet's expression darkened, and Elizabeth saw anger there in how he pressed his mouth into a tight line, his eyes narrowing. He did not speak for several moments, and Elizabeth wondered if he was trying to decide whether to be angry with her or with Mr. Darcy.

Finally, Mr. Bennet said, "The cad." He looked over at the grandfather clock and said, "The utter reprobate. Despite your mother's admonitions that I fail to understand the importance of a young lady's reputation, I know well enough not to storm to

Netherfield this instance and insist on pistols at dawn, but let me assure you, Mr. Fitzwilliam Darcy will make this right."

Elizabeth swallowed hard, feeling as though her throat were lined with cotton. Her father's words seemed to echo in the room, sending a shiver down her spine. "Mr. Darcy has already made his intentions clear," she said softly. "The banns will be read on Sunday and the two thereafter."

"I suppose we must make a show of it until a solution can be found. But I will speak with Mr. Darcy on the morrow. And rest assured, if Mr. Darcy cannot ensure your happiness, you will not have to endure a lifetime of misery against your will. On that, you have my word."

Her father's vehemence frightened her, though she knew it was born of love. Elizabeth did not know what Mr. Darcy intended for their marriage, but if Elizabeth broke the engagement, no other man would have her, and even if they did, her mother would never forgive her for throwing away such a magnificent match.

"Thank you, Papa," she said softly. "But I am sure

Mr. Darcy intends to honor his vows in spirit and letter."

"We shall see about that," Mr. Bennet muttered darkly as he rose from his seat and crossed to the bookshelf. "Now, it is late, and we both have much to consider. No matter what comes of this, you are my daughter, Lizzy. And we will see things right."

CHAPTER FOUR

Darcy had always found balls tedious, but the end of the Netherfield ball was excruciating. He barely endured the whispers and stares, the false wishes of congratulations as each guest took their leave, all while Miss Bingley's angry gaze bore into him like a dagger at his back.

Only after the last guest departed was Darcy able to breathe again. He allowed Bingley to lead him to the study. The scent of worn leather and wood polish enveloped him as they entered the paneled room.

Bingley went to retrieve the brandy, the decanter clinking softly as he poured two generous glasses. He pressed one into Darcy's hand before taking a seat in one of the leather chairs before the crackling fire.

Darcy sank into the other chair, the heat from the flames prickling his face. He swirled the brandy, inhaling its mellow aroma before taking a bracing sip. The liquor burned smoothly down his throat, but did little to calm his roiling thoughts.

He could still taste Miss Elizabeth on his lips, feel the softness of her skin against his fingertips as he'd tangled his fingers through her curls.

"Well," Bingley said, taking a long sip from his glass. "That was unexpected."

Darcy choked on a brandy flavored laugh.

"I did not know you and Miss Elizabeth were so close," Bingley continued, his tone light but with an underlying note of confusion. "When did you become engaged?"

"You witnessed it," Darcy said, taking another, longer gulp of his drink. The heat of it burned down his throat and into his chest.

Bingley's expression darkened, and for a moment, he looked almost angry, his open, cheerful face clouding over as his brows drew together. "And you and Miss Elizabeth came to some accord, then, while her sister was ill. Darcy, you have always been a true friend. Acerbic in your opinions, but true. You have made little secret that you believe my interest in Miss Bennet to be, as you termed it, a mere 'infatuation,' and yet you keep this from me?"

More than anger, Darcy realized Bingley was hurt. And he had a right to be. For Darcy to have chastised his friend for thinking to rush into an engagement with a young lady he barely knew, only to turn around and do the same thing himself...

Worse than the same thing. Darcy had disgraced himself and struck a terrible blow to Miss Elizabeth's reputation in the process.

Darcy sighed heavily, rubbing his hand over his face in frustration. He could not explain his actions. The only honorable thing to do after was to insist upon an engagement, which he had done. But while Miss Elizabeth had returned his kiss with passion, marriage was another matter entirely. "It was a moment of madness," Darcy said at last, his voice thick with emotion.

Bingley raised an eyebrow. "The kiss or the proposal?"

"Perhaps I am still abed, and this whole thing is a nightmare or a fever dream." Darcy took another sip of brandy and placed it on the side table before holding his arm out to his friend. "Pinch me and wake us both."

Bingley laughed, but there was little humor in it. "Well, if nothing else, this will surely put an end to my sister's hopes of winning your favor. That, at the least, will bring me peace."

"Miss Bingley and I do not suit." Darcy might have suffered a moment of madness when he kissed Miss Elizabeth, but he knew his own mind well enough to know he and Miss Bingley were incompatible in all but the most surface manners.

"I love my sister, but you and her would tear each other to bits like two tomcats in a bag," Bingley agreed dryly, leaning back in his chair. "I only pray you and Miss Elizabeth can find some happiness together. She certainly does not lack wit or spirit, which is fortunate. I do not think you could stand a dull-witted woman, no matter her accomplishments.

And one who yielded to your every dictate would become equally tiresome."

"Dictates? Hardly! I only offer practical advice when necessary. I am no tyrant," Darcy protested, though he knew his friend had some right in it. Darcy held himself to high standards, and he expected others to do the same. He took another swallow of brandy, savoring the warm bite on his tongue.

Bingley laughed, this time with genuine amusement. He stretched his legs out before the fire. "Perhaps it was some instinct of your soul then, begging you to shed the bonds of propriety and allow room for your heart."

Darcy snorted derisively. "My soul is hardly so romantic."

Bingley shrugged. "What other explanation can there be? You have made no secret of your disdain for Miss Elizabeth's lack of accomplishments or connections, and yet you kissed her as if she were Aphrodite herself."

Darcy's face flamed. "I did not intend—" He stopped, realizing his denial would only make things worse. He had kissed Miss Elizabeth with a passion that had shocked him as much as anyone. "I kissed her because... because..." Darcy's voice trailed off as he struggled to find the words to explain what had happened.

"I suppose I should not be surprised," Bingley continued, taking another sip from his glass. "You are a man of strong passions, Darcy. You simply hide them well. But if you have genuine regard for Miss Elizabeth beyond passion, and if you wish for future happiness together, you would do well to seek the romance you find lacking in your soul. Else your rash decision will lead to nothing but misery."

Bingley's words weighed in Darcy's mind as both gentlemen drained and refilled their glasses, and Bingley shifted the subject to the eldest Bennet and the subject of his affections. Bingley knew Darcy well enough to give his friend time to thoroughly digest his advice. Though the rashness of his actions still baffled him, it forced Darcy to admit to himself that Miss Elizabeth had occupied his thoughts more than he'd liked after her stay at Netherfield. Her wit and spirit had impressed him, and even before their dance, his gaze had sought her out.

"We must, to bed," Bingley finally said, yawning.

"Fear not, old chap," he added with a smile. "Now that you and she are officially engaged, you can show your affections more directly." Bingley's cheeks, already reddened by alcohol, seemed to deepen as he ran a palm over his forehead. "Or perhaps less directly. Write her a poem."

Darcy snorted derisively. "I assure you, I have no talent for poetry."

"You are certainly quick enough to criticize my attempts." Bingley wrinkled his nose. "But if not poetry, give her one of your sketches. You have more than a fair hand, as much as you deny it."

"She is likely fonder of literature."

"Then embarrass yourself in verse. You can do no worse with it than you have with wooing." Bingley stood, stretching his arms overhead. "The brandy is in the cabinet if you wish for another nightcap." He gestured to the intricately carved mahogany cabinet in the corner, the brandy decanter visible through the glass doors.

"But I suggest you get some rest." Bingley yawned again, running a hand through his tousled hair, limned in the reflection of orange firelight. "We will probably be receiving some number of Bennets on the morrow, and it would be best they do not find you in your cups."

Darcy forced a smile, to which Bingley returned an exaggerated expression of surprise, and after exchanging another round of pleasantries, Bingley left. Darcy leaned back into the heavy leather of the chair, closing his eyes as he tried to imagine what Miss Elizabeth might say to him upon her next visit. She had seemed shocked by his kiss, but she had not resisted.

He felt a stirring of desire at the memory of her lips against his and quashed it. His body thrummed with energy. The energy of memory, guilt, and desire. He stood, drained his remaining glass and, leaving it on the end-table, started down the corridor towards his rooms.

The corridor was dimly lit, with flickering sconces lining the walls every few feet. He was halfway between the study and his rooms when he heard low-pitched voices and the sound of a muffled sob.

Was it a servant? Or Miss Bingley, suffering a heart-break? Darcy hoped it was not the latter. He may not have had any marital interest in Bingley's sister, but he did not wish her ill.

"You have ruined everything!" a woman hissed. "How could you? You irredeemable fool!"

Darcy froze as he recognized Miss Bingley's shrill tones. Eavesdropping was ungentlemanly, but calling attention to himself while Miss Bingley was roundly chastising her lady's maid would only make things worse.

He could just glimpse their shadowed forms around the corner. Miss Bingley's figure was rigid with anger, while the maid cowered under her mistress's verbal lashing.

"Mistress!" the second woman pled, her voice thick. "Miss, I swear I didn't mean to! I only wanted—"

"You only wanted what?" Miss Bingley snapped. "Your Mr. Beaumont promised me his concoction would work! And instead, Mr. Darcy—with that—!"

What concoction, Darcy wondered, suspicion rising within him.

As he strained to listen, Miss Bingley seemed to take control of her temper, and her tone became more even as she said, "I will speak with Mr. Beaumont again. There must be some means to salvage this. Perhaps if there was a mistake in the dosage..." Miss Bingley's voice trailed off, and she let out a long sigh.

"Yes! Mistress!" the maid sniffled. "I cannot believe Mr. Beaumont would deceive you so—!"

"Best trust he finds some way to rectify his error. Else I will have no choice but to dismiss you from my service for recommending such a man."

The maid let out a strangled cry of protest as Miss Bingley continued, "Now go to bed. And do not breathe a word of this to anyone. You have done enough damage already. I will not allow you to cause more."

With that, Miss Bingley turned on her heel and, to Darcy's horror, started down the corridor towards him. He had only a moment to compose himself before she rounded the corner.

Miss Bingley froze, her eyes widening in shock and fear. "Mr. Darcy!"

"Miss Bingley," Darcy gave her a cool nod. "I thought

I was the only one troubled enough to be wandering about so late at night."

"I hope you did not hear anything... untoward. My newest maid has been proving herself less than satisfactory," Miss Bingley said, smoothing her hands over her skirts in a nervous gesture. "It is important to take a firm hand in these situations, you understand."

"I see," Darcy replied.

"Margaret will not be over-starching my gowns again," Miss Bingley added with a nervous giggle. "But you are not the sort to stand listening at keyholes, Mr. Darcy. I am sure you have far more pressing matters on your mind. Such as your engagement with Miss Eliza Bennet." Her lips twisted into a sneer as she uttered Elizabeth's name. "Miss Eliza is what some other ladies of the village call her. Such a quaint moniker, is it not? I had known Miss Eliza had only country manners, but I did not think her more uncouth than even her mother."

Darcy felt anger flare within him at Miss Bingley's words. He knew well enough from his own observations that Miss Elizabeth was a young woman of wit and spirit, but he had also observed her gentleness and care for her sister during Jane's illness, and how she had humored said mother's foibles without complaint.

"My fiancée is a lady of great intelligence and compassion," Darcy replied cooly. "I would suggest you do not speak so ill of her again in my presence."

"You hardly know her!" Miss Bingley protested, her voice rising sharply. She clasped her hands as if in supplication, the many rings on her fingers glinting in the candlelight. "It is not true emotion you feel, merely the effects of—!" She stopped herself, pressing a hand over her mouth. "She has bewitched you! I am sure of it!"

Darcy frowned. If not for the damning snatches of conversation he had just overheard, he would think the shock of Mr. Darcy's engagement had driven Miss Bingley to some form of madness. Darcy wanted to ask her about Mr. Beaumont, but if he pushed the conversation now, Miss Bingley would laugh it off and pretend ignorance. Better to approach Margaret when her mistress was absent. Considering Miss Bingley's treatment of the maid,

Darcy might be able to tempt the truth out of her with an offer of better employment.

"Perhaps," Darcy replied mildly, though he was certain any bewitching had not come from Miss Elizabeth. "But we are engaged to wed. And I am tired. It has been a long and troubling evening."

"Troubling indeed," Miss Bingley echoed, a speculative gleam entering her gaze. "Goodnight, Mr. Darcy," she said with a shallow curtsy, her eyes bright as she added, "I wish you sweet dreams."

Darcy nodded, though he harbored little hope for a peaceful sleep while this mystery remained. Bidding Miss Bingley goodnight, he strode swiftly toward his chambers, determined to uncover the truth about Mr. Beaumont and his suspicious "concoction."

CHAPTER FIVE

To Elizabeth's surprise, when she crept into her and Jane's shared bedroom, Jane had blown the lantern out, leaving only a single, sputtering candle. It cast flickering shadows over her too-still form, who breathed too regularly in the slow, steady rhythm of feigned sleep.

Elizabeth sighed heavily as she slipped off her gown and stays, scrubbing a damp cloth over her face and neck before slipping into her nightclothes and laying back onto the duvet. "Jane," she called out.

Jane let out a small exhalation.

"I know you are awake."

Jane shifted, pulling at the duvet. Finally, she whispered, her voice thick with emotion, "You could have told me. All this time, I was pouring out my heart to you about Mr. Bingley, and you were engaging in a secret courtship with a gentleman you clearly despised. Or...a gentleman you said you despised, though I suppose you did not say that exactly."

"I didn't—"

"Despise him, clearly not."

"No!" Elizabeth fisted the duvet in frustration. "I hid nothing from you. May lightning strike me dead at this moment if I am lying in this. There was no secret courtship!"

"But surely—" Jane began.

Elizabeth sat up, twisting around so she could look Jane in the eye. Her sister's face was barely visible in the dim light, but Elizabeth could see the hurt there in the slight downturn of her lips. "I do not know what happened, but until the moment Mr. Darcy kissed me, I had no notion of his interest." In a whisper, she added, "Or my own."

That was the oddest part of it. If his attentions had

been unwelcome, Elizabeth would have pushed him away and slapped him for good measure. Her reputation might have suffered, but this was Hertfordshire, her home, not an esteemed establishment like Almack's. The gentry would have taken her side if she had made her disapprobation clear. But Elizabeth had felt no distaste. She had melted into his embrace like a cat in a sunbeam. She had relished his touch. Wanted it. Wanted him. The desire had caught her as much off guard as the kiss itself.

And truthfully, after the act, Mr. Darcy had appeared just as surprised by his actions as Elizabeth. His shock had been genuine, as had his immediate step to rectify the situation. Mr. Darcy might have been many things: arrogant, judgmental, and impulsive if the kiss offered any sign, but he was not a cad.

"Oh, Lizzy," Jane said, leaping up from the bed and crossing the four steps between their beds.

Elizabeth felt tears prick at the corners of her eyes as Jane wrapped her in a warm embrace. She smelled of sweet orange and lingering candle-smoke, and Elizabeth breathed in deeply, feeling some of the tension ease from her shoulders. Despite her father's words, fearing Elizabeth had followed too closely in his footsteps by allowing passion to run her into an unhappy marriage, at least she had mended things with Jane.

"It is so strange, though, Lizzy. You are not Lydia to allow a flirtation to go too far. And Mr. Darcy has always seemed more dour than passionate in temperament. I remember Miss Bingley served those small pastries, and certain mushrooms can bring about a feverish state. But I cannot imagine Mr. Darcy succumbing to such a thing—unless he was truly ill and confused? Oh! Could that be it? If Mr. Darcy was suffering from a fever—"

"Then I also must have suffered from the same fever," Elizabeth said. And perhaps she had. Mr. Darcy's touch had certainly heated her desire. But no. She had only partaken in a glass of punch. As had Mr. Darcy.

Elizabeth's mind again shifted to that odd moment where Miss Bingley had stumbled, and the trick of the light had made Elizabeth question if Miss Bingley had put something in Mr. Darcy's drink.

Had she?

The thought seemed nearly as mad as the kiss itself,

and the fact that now Elizabeth was due to marry a gentleman she barely knew and was not even certain she tolerated outside of a single kiss. Though that kiss, she admitted, had been more than tolerable.

"What is it?" Jane asked. "You stiffened up, just now."

"This may sound odd, but..." Elizabeth shook her head.

Jane rubbed a slow circle with her palm over Elizabeth's arm. "I think nothing else could be more strange than what has already occurred."

Elizabeth laughed. "Fair." She took a breath. And another. And whispered so softly that Jane had to lean in to hear her, "I cannot be sure of what I saw... But I think Miss Bingley might have done something to Mr. Darcy's drink."

Jane frowned, tilting her head in confusion. "Done what?"

Elizabeth explained the strange moment she had witnessed when Miss Bingley stumbled, and how Elizabeth had thought and then dismissed the notion that the lady had dropped something into Mr. Darcy's glass.

. . .

"But surely not! I know you are not fond of Miss Bingley, but what reason would she have to poison her brother's friend and guest?"

The idea sounded even more far-fetched coming from Jane's mouth. And yet, Elizabeth couldn't shake the certainty that she had seen something important. But even if Miss Bingley had dosed Mr. Darcy's punch with something—a mushroom perhaps?—it did little to explain Elizabeth's reaction. She remembered the sweet taste of him on her lips after his first kiss. That had tasted nothing like mushrooms. Elizabeth continued, "I do not know why she would do such a thing." But as she spoke, she realized the 'why' was the least opaque part of this entire mess.

Miss Bingley was clearly enamored of Mr. Darcy, and though Elizabeth knew little of the gentleman's feelings for Caroline Bingley beyond his disdain for her flirtations, he had been notably cool towards Miss Bingley during Elizabeth's stay at Netherfield. How far would Miss Bingley go to secure Mr. Darcy's interest if she thought herself in love with the gentleman? Or, less charitably, in love with his ten-thousand a year?

"Jane, you know more about plants and herbs than I do. And you get on well with the apothecary. Can you ask if Mr. Jones knows of any draughts that might cause such behavior as what happened tonight?" Elizabeth ran her tongue over her lips and her cheeks warmed. "Something sweet."

"

Jane shook her head. "You are understandably distraught, Lizzy, but I still cannot believe Miss Bingley would do such a thing! She may not be the most amiable woman, but surely, she would not stoop to such depths."

"Perhaps not," Elizabeth allowed, though her brief interactions with the lady had shown Miss Bingley to be a cunning and ambitious woman who would go to great lengths to secure what she wanted. And while Elizabeth knew little of Mr. Darcy beyond his looks, his wealth, and his disdain for those less fortunate than himself, he did not seem a man easily swayed by flirtations alone. But Jane was too kind-hearted to see the worst in others, even when their faults were obvious. Elizabeth loved her sister dearly for that, but it also meant Jane was sometimes too trusting. "I know I sound like Lydia, seeing plots and intrigues where there are none. And it is possible the poisoning, if there was a poisoning, happened by accident. If so, it is even more important we find out what could have caused it. Lest someone else suffer the same effects, or worse."

"I suppose," Jane agreed, though she sounded unconvinced. "If you truly believe this to be important... I will ask Mr. Jones about it tomorrow. But you must promise not to do anything rash until we learn more about if something like this is even possible. You cannot accuse Miss Bingley, or anyone, of such a thing without proof. Please Lizzy. I do not wish to make an enemy of the Bingleys."

Even if Elizabeth was one to make accusations without evidence, the undisguised fear in her sister's voice would have ensured Elizabeth's silence. Her kiss and sudden engagement had already caused Jane enough pain and confusion. Jane's affection for Mr. Bingley had only grown since his arrival in Hertfordshire, and Elizabeth did not wish to cause her sister any more distress than she already had.

"You have my word," Elizabeth said firmly. It would be foolish and cruel to make an accusation of that sort without evidence. But if Elizabeth found proof of wrongdoing on Miss Bingley's part, she would have to speak up. Elizabeth wanted a marriage grounded in genuine affection. How could such a future be born of a lie?

CHAPTER SIX

Darcy had just himself in the breakfast nook with a cup of coffee, considering how he might call on Miss Bingley's maid without alerting the lady to his intentions, when he heard carriage wheels and the clip-clop-thud of horses' hooves outside.

Mr. Hurst looked up from his plate of eggs, sausage, and kippers with bleary eyes. "Who is that so early?" He yawned, glaring out the window.

Darcy followed his gaze, wincing as the bright morning sunlight pierced through his lingering headache. The lace curtains obscured much of the view, but he could make out enough to recognize the modest Bennet carriage approaching up the drive.

Sunlight glinted off its worn blue paint and oxidized brass fittings. One wheel looked dangerously close to needing repairs.

"I believe the Bennets," Darcy replied dryly, taking another sip from his mug. The events of the previous night felt like a strange dream in the aggressively cheerful light of morning. He had hoped, by sending a footman to inquire of the Bennets the best time to call, he would have time to clear the effects of the brandy from his head and get Margaret's side of the story concerning this mysterious concoction Miss Bingley had been so furious about. But the Bennets clearly kept country hours, and Darcy, already not fond of mornings, had clearly sent the footman too late.

"You asked them here?"

"Not exactly. But I cannot send them away."

"Indeed." Mr. Hurst glanced down at his morning clothes, which, while not as rumpled as they could have been, were still less than presentable. "I suppose I ought to go change then," he said, glancing down at his half-eaten breakfast with an expression of irritation. "But if I do not finish this now, I will have to wait until luncheon to eat again."

"I will receive them in the parlor." Darcy took a long sip from his coffee, trying to steel himself for what was likely to be a difficult conversation.

"Messy business, this," Mr. Hurst muttered around a mouthful of sausage. "Engagements. And you certainly made a spectacle of things." He chuckled, adding, "I do not envy you."

Darcy did not envy himself either. He had not come with Bingley to Netherfield with the thought of marriage or even courtship. And while a light hum of excitement seemed to simmer under his skin at the thought of seeing Miss Elizabeth again, he could not deny that he was also nervous.

He had kissed her in full view of the entire room, and then, when he realized the seriousness of his actions, he had proposed marriage with no prior courtship or even an offer to call upon her family. The memory of Elizabeth's lips against his lingered like an aged scotch on his tongue, and Darcy wondered what it might be like to kiss her again. To hold her in his arms, feel her body pressed against his. But he knew little else about her, beyond her wit, love of reading, and kindness towards her sister. That alone did not a marriage make.

Darcy's stomach churned with unease. Worse, he had little idea how Miss Elizabeth might react now that the shock of his actions had worn off. Would she be angry? Or worse, would she be indifferent? The thought of her fine eyes regarding him coolly made his steps falter.

A footman entered, bowing low as he said, "Mr. Bennet and his daughters have arrived, sir."

"Bring them to the parlor," Darcy ordered.

The footman bowed again and took his leave as Mr. Hurst shoveled another forkful of eggs into his mouth.

Darcy finished his coffee in two long swallows and rose to his feet. "Enjoy your breakfast," he said to Mr. Hurst, who grunted in reply as Darcy left the room.

The parlor was a pleasingly appointed room with a high ceiling and large windows that let in ample light with walls papered in a pale green pattern and adorned with several landscape paintings. As Mr.

Darcy settled himself on one of the plush chairs, he heard footsteps outside the door and braced himself for what was likely to be an uncomfortable conversation. He only had a few moments to enjoy the sounds of birdsong from outside before the door opened, and Mrs. Bennet swept into the room in a swirl of skirts, practically bowling over the footman in her haste, her cheeks flushed and her expression bright with excitement.

"Mr. Darcy! How good it is to see you this morning!" She clasped her hands in front of her chest and beamed at him. "This is a most lovely room! So well appointed. And this chair! So soft and comfortable. Such lovely brocade! I am sure you have many visitors who appreciate its comforts." Mrs. Bennet had not even taken a seat, but she ran her hand over the fabric as if she were trying to memorize every thread.

"Mrs. Bennet," Darcy said, rising to his feet as behind their mother, Elizabeth and Jane entered the room, followed by Mr. Bennet. Elizabeth's eyes met Darcy's for an instant, and he felt his pulse quicken.

"Oh, Mr. Darcy, no need for such formality. You may, if you wish, call me Mama. It is as all of our girls do.

And Miss Charlotte Lucas. She is plain, but a kind girl. And soon it will be my and Mr. Bennet's pleasure to call you son!"

Behind her mother, Elizabeth's face lost all color. "Mama!" she hissed.

Mrs. Bennet showed no signs of hearing her daughter. She barreled onwards. "I have always known my girls would make magnificent matches, but I never dreamed—"

Elizabeth grabbed her mother's arm. "Please!"

Mrs. Bennet looked over at her second daughter, her brows furrowing in confusion. "Whatever is the matter with you?"

Mr. Bennet, who had been observing the scene with a grim expression much at odds with the wryly amused demeanor Darcy had observed during his previous interactions with the man, cleared his throat loudly. "I had hoped for a moment of your time." Mr. Bennet glanced at his wife. "Alone."

"Alone?" Mrs. Bennet's eyes widened. "Surely whatever you say to Mr. Darcy can be repeated in front of his betrothed and her sister. We will be a family soon, and it is only proper—"

"It is only proper I speak with the gentleman who would ask for my daughter's hand," Mr. Bennet interrupted, his tone firm.

The door opened, and Bingley strode in. "Mr. Bennet," he nodded to the gentleman, who returned the gesture with stiff politeness. "Mrs. Bennet," Bingley turned to Elizabeth's mother, who seemed torn between outrage and delight at the attention. "Miss Bennet, Miss Elizabeth." He bowed to each in turn, his gaze lingering on Jane, who blushed prettily as she returned his greeting.

Bingley seemed oblivious to the tension between Darcy and Mr. Bennet, though Darcy knew from the slight tightening of his friend's mouth that he had noticed it. "Mrs. Bennet, I had hoped we might take a walk around the grounds if you are so inclined," Bingley continued brightly. "The weather is fine, and I have heard much of your Miss Bennet and Miss Elizabeth's love of nature."

Bless you, Bingley, Darcy thought, his gaze meeting his friend's as Mrs. Bennet exclaimed with delight,

"Oh, Jane is very fond of gardens, and Netherfield has such lovely ones! And Lizzy is fond of walking. And it will certainly give the three of us the chance to get better acquainted."

"I would not presume to escort your daughters unchaperoned," Bingley said smoothly.

Mrs. Bennet gave a start and then let out a laugh that was a touch too loud. "Oh! Of course! You are such a gentleman! I had nearly forgotten myself. But I am sure my girls would enjoy your company. Would you not?" She turned towards Elizabeth and Jane, who both nodded in agreement.

Bingley gave Darcy a nod, and Darcy was certain his friend's left eyelid lowered slightly in a barely perceptible wink. He then offered his arm to Mrs. Bennet, who took it with a giggle that made her sound like a much younger woman. "Mr. Bingley, I cannot be the Bennet whose arm you most wish to offer, but I am sure my girls will forgive my temporary usurpation."

"I assure you, Mrs. Bennet, there is no usurping involved," Bingley said gallantly as he led Mrs. Bennet out of the room, her daughters walking behind. Miss Elizabeth looked back over her shoulder, catching Darcy's gaze. There was a tension around her eyes and mouth he did not like. He wanted to reassure her, but she turned away before he could think how to do so.

"Well then," Mr. Bennet said dryly after the door closed behind them. "Shall we speak plainly?"

"I would not have it any other way," Darcy replied. "My intentions towards your daughter are honorable, sir."

Mr. Bennet snorted derisively. "Is that so? Then I suppose rumors of your amorous behavior just last night, in full view of all the guests at Netherfield, were exaggerated."

Darcy's face heated. "I will admit my actions were impulsive—"

"Impulsive?" Mr. Bennet's voice rose sharply.

"I did not intend—"

Mr. Bennet held up a hand, cutting him off midsentence. "I am sure you did not," Mr. Bennet said dryly, his tone making it clear he did not believe Darcy's words in the slightest. "But you intended to ask for my daughter's hand in marriage, and yet you made no attempt to do so before now."

"I was overcome by emotion," Darcy said, his face flushing hotter as he realized how ridiculous that sounded. He struggled for some sensible explanation that neither seemed a fit of madness nor offered insult. "When Miss Elizabeth was at Netherfield during her sister's illness, I grew increasingly fond of her company." As Darcy spoke, he realized the truth of his words. He had admired her wit and intelligence, and though she lacked the accomplishments and connections that a woman of his status required, he could not deny that he had enjoyed her company more than any other lady he had met.

Mr. Bennet raised an eyebrow. "And yet, you did not think to call on us before now?"

"I did not wish to presume," Darcy replied stiffly. "I would not have offered for her if I had not intended to honor my vows."

Mr. Bennet snorted again, but this time with less heat. "I suppose that is something." He crossed to the window and peered out at the grounds where Bingley was leading Mrs. Bennet and her daughters towards the gardens. "You are a very wealthy gentle-man," Mr. Bennet said. "And for many, that would be enough. But my Elizabeth has always dreamed of finding affection in her marriage, not just security."

"I understand," Darcy said, though he was unsure how much he did. Bingley was the sort who sang of love in his cups and composed verse on leftover scraps of foolscap, believing it a necessary part of courtship. Darcy had never thought much about love in his own marriage, assuming it would follow naturally after the wedding. Or not. It hardly mattered so long as he produced an heir. His parents had been fond of each other, but neither had been demonstrative in their affections. "I cannot promise love, but I can promise respect and honor."

"That is something," Mr. Bennet said again, though he still sounded skeptical. "I will not deny my daughter the chance for happiness, and with circumstances as they are, your proposal, and her acceptance, have saved her from ruin. Lizzy does not blame you for what happened, so I cannot. But I do not wish to see her suffer. And for my Lizzy, a life of duty without affection would be a miserable one."

Darcy nodded. He was uncertain what he felt for

her. It was all too sudden, too unexpected, and he knew little of Miss Elizabeth beyond the brief time they had spent together at Netherfield. But he could not deny the lady had stirred something within him he had not felt before. Something warm and tender and exciting. "I will do my best to ensure her happiness," he promised, hoping he could keep it, somehow.

Mr. Bennet gave Darcy a long, measuring look. "See that you do, Mr. Darcy." He rolled his shoulders. "See that you do."

CHAPTER SEVEN

After their conversation with Mr. Darcy, Elizabeth and Jane walked through the garden alongside their mother and Mr. Bingley. As always, Mr. Bingley was charming and amicable, despite the deluge of Mrs. Bennet's churning chatter.

Elizabeth's thoughts swirled around the conversation Mr. Darcy was having with her father. She tried to calm her racing heart, knowing she would be no use to anyone if she continued to be such a bundle of nerves. The sweet scent of grass and honeysuckle wafted towards her on a gentle breeze, and she breathed in deeply, grateful for the respite the outdoors always brought.

Mrs. Bennet stepped back suddenly, causing Mr.

Bingley to stumble a little on the uneven path. "Mrs. Bennet?"

"Oh, my dear Mr. Bingley," Mrs. Bennet said, her voice rising as she grasped his arm with both hands. "You must forgive me! A full night of dancing has made my legs quite weary. I must rest for a minute. But our Jane would surely enjoy your conversation. Is that not right, Jane? Do tell our Mr. Bingley what a gentleman you find him to be, for I cannot fault his manners for a moment."

Jane's cheeks reddened, and she pressed a hand to her mouth. "Oh, Mama!"

"Oh Mama, nothing! Lizzy and I will be just a bit behind. Mr. Bingley, please, care for my Jane for me for a short while."

Elizabeth suppressed a sigh. Her mother was perfectly healthy and hardly out of breath. Mrs. Bennet's suggestion that Jane, and Mr. Bingley should continue the tour of the gardens without her was no doubt an attempt to further her daughter's romantic prospects, laudable but far too obvious in Elizabeth's estimation. On the other hand, her sister tended towards the 'far too subtle,' so perhaps there was some utility to her mother's machinations.

"They make a handsome couple," Mrs. Bennet said with a sigh, clasping her hands together as she watched Jane and Mr. Bingley walk ahead. "Do you not think so, Lizzy? Jane has such a delicate spirit, but her heart can withstand any storm. Your temperament is, in some ways, the opposite. I admit, I did worry about you. Your fire burns so brightly. But with a powerful man's support, like Mr. Darcy, you will flourish."

"I am glad you approve, Mama." Elizabeth said with a coolness to her tone that her mother neither acknowledged nor seemed to recognize.

"You have done very well for yourself, Lizzy. Better than I ever expected, in truth." Mrs. Bennet beamed at her second daughter, her expression bright with pride. "And Mr. Darcy is so handsome! No matter his initial reserve, his affections must be true if he has done as much to secure you! Perhaps this marriage will be the start of a new era for Longbourn. Jane is well on her way to matrimony, so it is only the three youngest who need to find husbands."

Mrs. Bennet breathed out an overlong sigh. "What a pity Kitty and Mary did not join us as well! The gentlemen here are as plentiful for plucking as the fruits of Mr. Phillips's old apple tree in autumn. But Mr. Bennet would have none of it. He almost made as if to send me from the carriage, and you know your father is rarely so stern!" Mrs. Bennet shook her head. "And after everything that has happened!"

Elizabeth nodded, though she did not feel nearly as cheerful as her mother did. Her pulse pounded in her ears, and her body felt as if it were trembling. What must everyone think of her after such a display at the ball? After Mr. Darcy's declaration. Their engagement and her impending marriage seemed to loom over everything like an oncoming storm.

She touched the frayed ribbon adorning the sleeve of her gown. Mrs. Bennet had declared this morning they would need to order new gowns for the wedding, but Elizabeth was not ready to acknowledge that in less than a month she would be wed. She felt as if she were still spinning out of control from the previous night. And she could not forget the concern and fear she had seen in Mr. Darcy's eyes.

Mrs. Bennet continued, "And Lizzy, you must not forget! When you are married, you must recommend your sisters to Mr. Darcy's aunt, Lady Catherine de Bourgh. She—"

"Mrs. Bennet! Miss Elizabeth!"

Irritation quickly overtook Elizabeth's relief at the reprieve from her mother's stream of conversation as she recognized the figure approaching. Miss Caroline Bingley strode across the lawn, a parasol balanced on her left shoulder. Her skirts brushing over the dewy grass. The sun shone on her golden locks in a way that made her hair almost glow like an angel. But her expression was anything but angelic as she narrowed her eyes, surveying Mrs. Bennet and Elizabeth with a smile as false as a painted mask. "My brother neglected to inform me you were calling so early."

Mrs. Bennet trilled a laugh. "Miss Bingley! I am so delighted to see you! Your brother has been such a gentleman! And our Jane is so fond of gardens."

Miss Bingley gave Mrs. Bennet a cool nod. "She seems quite taken with... the garden. So many flowers blooming in her cheeks!" She gestured towards Jane, who was blushing prettily indeed as she and Mr. Bingley walked side by side, deep in conversation.

"And Miss Elizabeth," Miss Bingley purred. "May I offer my felicitations on your forthcoming marriage to Mr. Darcy?" She tilted her chin, nose wrinkling as she added, "Though it is hardly the match I would have thought him capable of."

"Capable of?" Mrs. Bennet asked, blinking in confusion. "What do you mean?"

Miss Bingley waved her gloved hand dismissively. "You must not mind me. I only meant to comment on how surprising it is, considering Mr. Darcy's particular tastes. He has always preferred women with more... connections. Though, of course, Miss Eliza is charming enough, in her own way."

A shock of rage flared through Elizabeth. She clenched her fists at her side as her cheeks flamed. "My engagement to Mr. Darcy is not a matter for you to criticize," she managed, her voice tight with anger. "If you have a grievance against me, I suggest you speak more directly."

Miss Bingley's eyes widened slightly, but her smile

only grew, and she tapped her parasol against her shoulder. "My! My! Miss Elizabeth, how fierce you are! Mr. Darcy must be so pleased with his catch!"

Elizabeth drew a shaky breath, determined not to slap Miss Bingley, though it was a near thing. "He is. And I am honored to have received his attentions."

Miss Bingley's nostrils flared. She reached out, her gloved hand hovering near Elizabeth's face as if she meant to caress her cheek. "You really are something, aren't you? Mr. Darcy must be truly dazzled by your... liveliness."

As Miss Bingley's fingers brushed Elizabeth's cheek, a familiar voice rang out from behind them. "Miss Elizabeth?"

Miss Bingley whirled around, dropping her hand to her side. Elizabeth looked over her shoulder to see Mr. Darcy approaching, her father at his side.

Elizabeth felt a fluttering in her belly as she saw Mr. Darcy. His coat was slightly rumpled, and his cravat seemed looser than usual. She wondered how his conversation with her father had gone and if Mr. Darcy had found Mr. Bennet's approval. He seemed less nervous than he had earlier, though there was a slight flush to his cheeks, which Elizabeth realized was anger from his tight mouth and furrowed brow. "Miss Bingley." Mr. Darcy gave a stilted bow. "I did not expect to see you up and about so early."

"Oh, in the country, one must keep country hours!" Miss Bingley simpered, pressing a hand to her chest as if to emphasize her point. "And it is such a lovely day! How could one bear to be cooped up inside?"

"Indeed," Darcy replied dryly. His gaze met Elizabeth's, and she could not help the warmth that passed through her at his look. She had thought Mr. Darcy handsome, but now, in the light of day, his features struck her even more vividly. His dark hair fell over his forehead in loose curls, and his eyes, though sharp, had a sweetness to them that caught Elizabeth off guard.

"Mr. Darcy!" Mrs. Bennet chirped, hurrying over to him and grasping his arm. "You look so handsome in the morning sun. I am sure you will agree, Miss Elizabeth!"

Elizabeth felt a sudden surge of panic at her mother's overweening and unmannered praise, but Miss Bingley replied before Elizabeth could speak, "Quite true! Mr. Darcy is a gentleman who understands the importance of looking his best, even in such a casual setting as a morning walk. And he is one who will not neglect propriety, no matter how trying the circumstances." Her gaze met Elizabeth's again, and Elizabeth felt a chill pass through her.

Mr. Darcy gently extricated himself from Mrs. Bennet's grip. "Miss Elizabeth," he said, ignoring Miss Bingley's remarks. "I had hoped to speak with you in private."

Miss Bingley's lips twisted, and a spark of fury glittered in her gaze.

"Perhaps Mr. Darcy and Miss Elizabeth may walk together while we await Jane and Mr. Bingley," Mrs. Bennet suggested, stepping between Miss Bingley and Elizabeth.

Mr. Darcy glanced over his shoulder to where Mr. Bennet had paused a short distance away, surveying the group with a hawklike gaze. Elizabeth followed his glance, noting that her father seemed more thoughtful than angry. Had he and Mr. Darcy reached an understanding? She did not dare hope for more.

"Indeed," Mr. Darcy agreed, moving to Elizabeth's side and offering his arm.

Elizabeth took it, acutely aware of Mr. Darcy's closeness. She felt the warmth radiating off him, even though there was a respectable distance between them. Miss Bingley sniffed indignantly and flicked open her parasol.

Mrs. Bennet hooked her arm through Miss Bingley's free one, practically dragging her away as she prattled, "Miss Bingley, you simply must show me Netherfield's gardens..."

Elizabeth and Mr. Darcy strolled arm in arm, silent except for the rustle of leaves and crunch of pebbles beneath their boots. The air between them felt thick with expectation. Elizabeth sensed Mr. Darcy's gaze on her, his breathing, slow and measured, as if he, too, were struggling for words. Finally, he said, "I hope you are well today. I feared, after what happened..."

"I am well, Mr. Darcy. Thank you." Elizabeth could not quite meet his gaze as she added, "And thank you for... taking the lead last night. It could have been much worse for me had you not."

Mr. Darcy stopped, turning to face her fully. "Miss Elizabeth, I am truly sorry for what happened. It was not my intent to behave in such a manner, but I cannot deny my actions. I only hope we can move forward in a manner that shows a mutual respect."

Elizabeth flushed, wishing she could express the conflicting emotions swirling through her. She was not angry with Mr. Darcy precisely, though she felt a ripple of irritation that he kept apologizing for kissing her, as if he regretted the kiss. Which was proper, and certainly, she should have regretted it. Her skin heated as she remembered the scratch of his stubble, the warmth of his breath, and the strength of his arms around her. She had heard the gasps of surprise, the whispers and murmurs, but his touch had so overwhelmed her, she had paid no heed to the rest. She should have regretted this even more in the too-bright sunlight, but, standing so close, Elizabeth could not deny the desire simmering inside her, or the thrill she felt in his presence.

And then there was the issue of Miss Bingley's actions. What Elizabeth had seen or thought she had seen. How could Elizabeth bring up such a subject of Miss Bingley dosing his drink?

"Mushrooms," Elizabeth blurted out.

"Excuse me?"

Elizabeth flushed harder. "Mushrooms. Jane and I recently had an interesting conversation about mushrooms. Some can make one... act strangely. Have you heard of such things, Mr. Darcy?"

Darcy stared at her for a moment, his eyebrows furrowing. "I cannot say I have," he said carefully. "But mushrooms can have curious properties. Some of the older goodwives in the village would gather them for their tables. It is a perilous task if you do not know what you are doing."

Elizabeth nodded, relieved she had broached the subject without making a fool of herself. "Yes, exactly. They can be dangerous. But it is something to consider." She trailed off, wishing she had a stronger argument.

"Do you believe mushrooms had something to do with our... behavior at the ball?" Mr. Darcy asked, expression surprisingly grim. His features were drawn, and his lips pressed tightly together as if he were holding something back some terrible suspicion.

Elizabeth hesitated, remembering Jane's advice. They had not spoken to the apothecary yet, and without proof, she would risk losing Mr. Darcy's good opinion or incurring Miss Bingley's wrath by accusing her of... what? But Mr. Darcy seemed willing to listen, and Elizabeth sensed there was more to his question than idle curiosity.

"Not mushrooms exactly." Elizabeth hesitated. "There are also certain bread grain molds, I've heard..." And how long did those effects last? After a night's sleep, even if Miss Bingley had given Mr. Darcy a dose, surely the effect should have faded by now. Nor should it have affected Elizabeth at all. And yet, she still wanted to kiss him. And what harm would it do? Elizabeth licked her lips, recalling Mr. Darcy's warm, sweet taste.

But Mr. Darcy's expression remained solemn, and he made no move to kiss her at all. "We have both had enough of deception, Miss Elizabeth," he said. "If there is anything you know or suspect, anything that might shed light on what happened, please, I beg you, share it with me."

Elizabeth's gaze locked with his, and she saw something flicker in his eyes, something like fear, and something like hope. Elizabeth's heartbeat quickened. And then, before she could change her mind, she leaned in and whispered, "I fear Miss Bingley might have put something in your drink at the ball."

CHAPTER EIGHT

D arcy stood stunned as Miss Elizabeth explained what she had witnessed at the Netherfield ball. It put the conversation he had over-heard between Miss Bingley and her maid Margaret into an entirely new light. Miss Bingley had truly dosed his drink? But why? To force his affection? Darcy shuddered, realizing what might have happened if he had succumbed.

Though he had succumbed to something.

Miss Elizabeth's fingertips rested lightly on his arm, his atop hers, a gesture well within the bounds of propriety. And yet Darcy could not ignore the thrill that passed through him at the contact. She was unlike any woman he had met before. Fiery and intelligent, with a wit that matched his own and a keen insight into human nature. And she smelled faintly of lavender and something uniquely herself, a scent that made Darcy want to press his nose to her neck and inhale deeply.

Yes, his attraction felt real, but how could he trust it? How could he trust himself?

He needed to find Margaret and find out the truth of what had happened.

"Tell me you do not think me mad? Or cruel?" Miss Elizabeth said, her voice cutting over his thoughts. "It may have been nothing. I do not wish to hurt Miss Bingley's reputation with unfounded accusations."

Darcy shifted closer, leaning down until he could feel Miss Elizabeth's warm breath on his face. "Never could I think you cruel, Miss Elizabeth."

Her eyes widened, and her lips parted, revealing the sweet curve of her pink tongue. Darcy fought the urge to lean in and taste her mouth, to capture her lips with his and lose himself in the passion he felt stirring in his soul. She was so beautiful, with her wide, dark eyes, her pert nose, and the soft curl of her brown hair. He wanted to run his hands through those locks, to pull her close and kiss her until they were both breathless and panting with no thought for propriety or anything beyond the moment.

"Mr. Darcy," Miss Elizabeth breathed. Her fingers tightened on his arm, and Darcy realized they had somehow drifted closer until there was barely an inch between their noses. Darcy swallowed hard, feeling a strange lump in his throat.

Miss Elizabeth's gaze flicked to his mouth, and Darcy thought he saw a flash of interest in her eyes. Desire? Or dreaming on his part?

Darcy felt as if he stood in the center of a thunderstorm, and lightning had just struck. He pulled away, trying to steady his breathing and ignore the want pulsing through his veins.

"Miss Elizabeth, your suspicions are not unfounded." Darcy described what he had overheard between Miss Bingley and her maid, Margaret. As he spoke, the color drained from Miss Elizabeth's face. She glanced towards Miss Bingley, who was still walking arm in arm with Mrs. Bennet, oblivious to what was transpiring.

"Mr. Darcy, that is serious. If Miss Bingley is guilty of such a thing, her actions could have lasting repercussions for us both."

Darcy nodded. He glanced over his shoulder at Mr. Bennet, who was watching them with a cool, assessing gaze. He still did not know how to fulfill his promise to Mr. Bennet, especially considering the duplicity that had put both him and Miss Elizabeth in this situation. And he still wanted her. If this attraction was because of a dosing in his drink, how long would it last?

"We cannot confront Miss Bingley directly," he said, turning back to Miss Elizabeth. "But if we investigate thoroughly, we might uncover something that will lend credence to our suspicions."

"It will make sense for us to work together," Miss Elizabeth said with a nod. "Given our sudden engagement."

"I will speak with Margaret as soon as I can meet with her apart from her mistress."

Miss Elizabeth glanced towards Miss Bingley again. "Mr. Bingley seems unaware of Miss Bingley's actions, but I do not think we can approach him about it. She is, after all, his sister."

"Yes," Darcy said grimly. He knew Bingley well enough to realize that while his friend was generous and well meaning, his blind spot regarding his sister's faults was considerable. "We will have to proceed with circumspection."

"At least, as we are engaged to wed, we can meet and share what we have learned. And maybe... maybe it will help. Somehow."

"I agree." Darcy forced a smile, though he felt a pang of something like disappointment in his chest. He enjoyed being with Miss Elizabeth, and even with the shadows of scandal hanging over them, he did not wish to part from her company. But if they somehow proved Miss Bingley was responsible for their passionate kiss, it changed nothing about the duty they both felt bound to perform. Duty and honor.

Darcy glanced at Elizabeth. Her expression was shuttered, but he sensed a flicker of the same uncertainty he felt. She was trying to hide it, but he could see the tension in her jaw and the tightening of her grip on his arm.

"I fear this is not the joyous occasion you would have wished for," he said. "But I hope that, in time, it will become so. It is not my wish to make you miserable."

Elizabeth nodded, her expression relaxing. "Thank you, Mr. Darcy. I had always hoped to marry for affection..."

Those were the exact words her father had spoken, and Darcy winced. "I understand," he said. "And I will do my utmost to ensure you are happy, Miss Elizabeth. I want that more than you know."

Her smile was genuine now, and Darcy's heart lifted. She was beautiful when she smiled. She made him wish he was a romantic at heart, like Bingley, who composed odes to Jane Bennet on every scrap of paper he could find. Suddenly, Darcy wanted to write poetry and shower Miss Elizabeth with gifts and adoration. But Darcy knew better than to pursue a passion that might be false, given the circumstances of their engagement.

"I know you are fond of reading," Darcy said, hoping

to offer her some sort of token of affection. "Perhaps I may gift you books from my library?"

"That is a kind thought."

"I have a rather extensive collection." Darcy flushed as he realized he had revealed too much, but Elizabeth only laughed, her eyes lighting with pleasure.

"Then perhaps you and I may yet become friends," she teased. Her lips quirked, and Darcy could not resist imagining kissing her again. Would that passion fade once Miss Bingley's machinations were undone? He hoped not. The stab of fear that pierced him at the thought of not wanting to kiss Miss Elizabeth surprised Darcy.

What had Miss Bingley done to him? He could not even trust his own emotions. Darcy took pride in his knowledge of self and his ability to make rational decisions based on his logic, but now he felt as if he was drowning in a sea of doubt.

"What books do you enjoy?" Elizabeth asked.

"Shakespeare," Darcy blurted out, grabbing at the first name that came to mind. "He is a favorite of mine. But I also read widely. Books on natural philosophy and science, as well as works of fiction. And I have a fondness for adventure stories."

"You? Adventure stories?"

"Are you saying you thought me dull?" His cheeks warmed.

Miss Elizabeth's eyes twinkled mischievously. "I would never presume so. Have you read Robinson Crusoe?"

"Several times. I am a great admirer of Defoe. My mother used to read it to me as a boy, and I still revisit it from time to time." Darcy did not mention how much as a child he had dreamed of setting off on an adventure, and how jealous he had been when his cousin Richard bought his commission and left for war. Darcy had stayed at home, studied, and dutifully fulfilled his obligations. Though he could not deny the occasional pang of envy when he heard of his acquaintances' escapades, Darcy was practical. He had responsibilities.

And now he had Miss Elizabeth. A responsibility? Or maybe a reward?

Elizabeth squeezed his arm. "Your mother seems like a delightful woman."

Darcy's chest ached as he thought of his mother's soft laughter and the smell of rosemary from her kitchen gardens. And the games she had made for him and George Wickham before the boy had grown sullen and distant, consumed by his resentment of their family. Darcy missed his mother every day, and though years had dulled the pain, it had never quite faded. "She was," he said. "Not every lady is truly fond of children, but she loved to spend time with us. She enjoyed silly games."

"Papa is the same." Miss Elizabeth grinned. "He says we are all frivolous, but when it comes time to play conundrums or cards, he is the most competitive."

"I can imagine. Mr. Bennet seems a formidable opponent." Darcy's gaze flitted to the gentleman in question who had joined his wife and Miss Caroline Bingley by the hedges.

Miss Elizabeth laughed, the sound light and joyous. A curl caught in the light breeze fluttered over her cheek. It was a bit wild, like her, and Darcy wanted to take it between his fingertips and hold it to his lips. He had desired no one like this, and it terrified him. Was this some lingering effect of Miss Bingley's actions, or his own true feelings? He had always scoffed at such nonsense, but now, faced with a woman he admired, and who, despite their circumstances, stirred his passion, he found himself at a loss.

"It seems we at least have one thing in common," Miss Elizabeth said, and Darcy realized he had let the silence between them grow too long. "We both enjoy books."

"Two things," Darcy said. "Books and adventures." It was three if he counted kissing, but he would not be so bold as to say that aloud.

Miss Elizabeth tilted her head slightly, her expression speculative. "True. Adventures." She spoke as if tasting the word, and Darcy felt heat flare in his loins at the way her tongue curled around it. He cleared his throat, embarrassed by his response, and Miss Elizabeth blinked as if coming out of a dream.

Was this passion he felt for her real?

"Two things, yes," Darcy managed. "We will have much to talk about during our walks."

Miss Elizabeth's smile broadened. "Indeed," she said.

As Miss Elizabeth and Darcy strolled arm in arm, Miss Elizabeth's eyes turned from him to her mother and Caroline Bingley. Darcy followed her gaze and saw the tension in Miss Elizabeth's jaw and the tightening of her grip on his arm.

"Three things. Books. Adventures, and a lifetime together." Miss Elizabeth's words settled between them, heavy and dense with implications. Her tone was somber, and Darcy could taste the tension in the air, dry and prickling, like a warning.

Darcy's heart sank. He knew Miss Elizabeth had no choice but to marry him. And while he would do everything in his power to make her happy, he could not deny the doubts clouding his heart. Had Miss Bingley's potion somehow altered his affections, or was this passion real? And would Miss Elizabeth come to regret marrying him, bound to a man she may have despised if it were not for the circumstances of their engagement?

"A happy lifetime," Darcy ventured and Miss Elizabeth nodded, though the smile she gave him was strained. She glanced towards Miss Bennet and Bingley, who seemed wrapped in their own world, oblivious to the rest of the party. Miss Bennet's eyes shone brightly, and Bingley grinned with genuine warmth.

A marriage based on affection. Was that not what Mr. Bennet had said his future bride most wanted? Darcy dredged his mind for a sonnet about love, and said, "Love looks not with the eyes, but with the mind, and therefore is wing'd Cupid painted blind."

Elizabeth's smile softened into something genuine. "I am uncertain Midsummer Night's Dream is the most appropriate work to quote at the present moment."

Darcy flushed and then a laugh escaped him, breaking the tension. "Perhaps not," he admitted. "But you must admit we find ourselves in a truly tangled web this morning."

Elizabeth snorted. "A tangled web indeed. More farce than fact, if I am honest. But Mr. Darcy, though it might seem otherwise, I am glad we are united in our efforts to unravel it, if spider's webs can even unravel." Her brow furrowed most adorably. "They tend more to cling, I believe."

"Mr. Darcy, Miss Elizabeth!" Miss Bingley's shrill voice cut through their conversation. "May I inquire what you find so amusing?"

Darcy stiffened as she approached, her parasol swinging at her side. Mr. and Mrs. Bennet trailed behind.

"Just discussing Shakespeare, Miss Bingley," Elizabeth said sweetly. "Are you fond of a Midsummer Night's Dream?"

The color drained from Miss Bingley's cheeks. "Not particularly, I am afraid," she said, her smile tight.

Darcy raised an eyebrow. Elizabeth's tone was teasing, but he could detect a note of anger beneath her words. She said, "It is an amusing tale."

"Is it?" Miss Bingley replied, her tone frosty. "I find it difficult to follow. All that business with fairies and elves. And that Puck fellow sounds positively wicked."

"Some would argue that is half the fun of it, Miss Bingley." Elizabeth tilted her chin slightly, her gaze never leaving Miss Bingley's face. "Though, in truth, I believe Shakespeare intends for us to laugh at the follies of humanity. And we have much to laugh about, do we not, Mr. Darcy?" She rested her fingers on Darcy's arm again, and he shifted slightly, pulling her closer.

Miss Bingley's nostrils flared.

"Darcy!" Bingley called with a wave, his voice jovial. Bingley and Miss Jane Bennet walked arm-in-arm up the garden path. Jane's cheeks glowed rosy in the crisp autumn air, her hair drifting in the breeze and her eyes sparkling as if she and Bingley had shared some secret joke.

Darcy could not help but feel a stab of jealousy at their ease with each other. They moved as if in harmony, with Jane's arm looped through Bingley's, and Bingley occasionally brushing her knuckles with his thumb in a gentle caress. Their closeness was clear in every line of their bodies, from the tilt of Bingley's head towards Jane, to the way her eyes sparkled as they gazed up at him.

Darcy wondered what it would be like to court Miss Elizabeth so openly, without the shadow of deception and deceit hovering over them. She deserved someone who could love her freely, who would write poems and sing songs in her honor. One who could trust in the truth of his emotions and enjoy a proper courtship, not one handled awkwardly in reverse as circumstances had forced them into.

He glanced at Miss Elizabeth, wishing he could ask for her hand properly. But as Mr. Bennet's gaze bore into his back, Darcy knew his duty was clear. A duty Miss Elizabeth shared, though he could not deny the spark of hope that flared in his chest. He sensed a kinship with her, an understanding that went beyond words. But was it real? Or was it just the result of Miss Bingley's machinations?

CHAPTER NINE

The way to Mr. Beaumont's wagon was even more wretched a second time. Clouds hung heavy in a half-mist shroud, obscuring the sky and dripping water onto Caroline's bonnet. The lane was muddy, and the slick earth squelched under her boots as she hurried along. Caroline shivered in her pelisse and pressed a hand to her stomach, wishing she could cast off the awful weight of failure that seemed to drag her down with every step. As Caroline slipped and staggered, she cursed the rain, the Netherfield ball, Mr. Darcy, Mr. Beaumont's false potion, and everything else that had conspired to bring her to this low point.

Where was this dratted wagon? It had not seemed so long a walk before.

Caroline shoved through a patch of weeds, nearly impaling her glove on a thorny bush, stumbled into a clearing where Mr. Beaumont's wagon awaited. Mr. Beaumont perched on the stairs of his cart, his legs crossed and his gaze fixed on the muddy ground. He wore the same ratty coat as before, and his boots were nearly caked with mud. Caroline wrinkled her nose in disgust. Mr. Beaumont looked up as she approached, and a smirk flitted over his lips. "Miss Bingley," he called out, his teeth flashing in his dark beard. "Back so soon?"

Caroline flushed and planted her hands on her hips. Her voice was sharp as she replied, "You did not give me what I paid for."

Mr. Beaumont raised an eyebrow. "Did you not use the potion successfully, Miss Bingley? I've heard an announcement of an engagement. That alone shows the potion worked as intended, does it not?"

Was this man a fool or touched in the head? Caroline tossed her curls. "It did not work as intended!

Mr. Darcy kissed that... that Bennet girl." Caroline spat out the words as if they were bitter as a mouthful of vinegar. She clenched her fists at her sides and stepped towards Mr. Beaumont, her chest tight with anger. "And not just any Bennet girl, but the most inferior of the lot. You sold me a defective product—"

Mr. Beaumont shrugged, cutting her off with a casual flick of his wrist. "Miss Bingley, this is hardly my fault. I told you before, my potions do not guarantee love. They merely reveal what lies beneath."

Caroline narrowed her eyes. "Then yours revealed incorrectly. I paid you good coin—"

"And what would you have me do with that? Refund you?" He reached into the pocket of his coat and pulled free a familiar leather purse. "If you insist—"

"I want no such thing," Caroline snapped. "Keep your coins. But I want a solution to set matters right. You must brew me a different concoction. Something that will compel Mr. Darcy to fall in love with me. Or at least forget that Bennet chit."

Mr. Beaumont sighed, running a hand through his

hair. "Miss Bingley, my potions do not work that way."

"The least you can do is make things right. Is that too much to ask?"

Mr. Beaumont sighed and rose awkwardly to his feet. His movements were slow and measured as he waved Caroline to follow. As he tilted his back towards her, the lantern light shone over his cheek, and Caroline noticed for the first time a scar there, pale and silvery, as if from a knife wound. A chill rippled through Caroline, and she suddenly wished she had brought someone with her.

No. It was ridiculous to think such a thing. She could handle Mr. Beaumont.

Caroline squared her shoulders and followed him into his wagon, her nostrils flaring as she took in the musky, damp air and the shelves laden with jars and vials. It was the same chaotic mess as before, with herbs spilling from baskets and papers pinned to the wall with pins and knives. And the tiny figures in bone perched amidst the mess on the shelves, one swathed in a handkerchief sized cape of golden silk.

Mr. Beaumont gestured to a bench tucked against

the far wall, and Caroline perched uncomfortably, smoothing her skirts with trembling fingers. She was about to speak when Mr. Beaumont tugged a cord, and a lamp flared to life, casting the interior of the wagon in a sickly yellow glow.

Caroline blinked, her eyes adjusting to the light. Mr. Beaumont rifled over the contents of a shelf. While it seemed untidy, there was a system to the peddler's seeming madness. She glimpsed labels on the jars and scraps of notes scribbled on torn bits of paper.

"Ah! Here we are!" Mr. Beaumont cried, reaching for a small jar containing a dark liquid that Caroline suspected was ink. He turned, uncorked it, dipped a stick of charcoal inside, and held it out to her.

The smell was sharp and sickly sweet, like overripe oranges. Caroline gagged as she tried to force the scent from her nose, but it clung to her tongue, making her lips tingle. "What is that?"

A loud series of knocks sounded at the wagon door. "Beaumont?" A man called out. "I was told this was a Mr. Beaumont's place."

Before Mr. Beaumont could answer, the door swung open, and Caroline stared as a handsome, fair-haired gentleman in the red uniform of an officer strode in.

The officer seemed vaguely nervous, gaze darting back and forth as if searching for something. Mr. Beaumont stared at him for a long moment, and Caroline shifted uncomfortably on the bench. Who was this man, and what business did he have with Mr. Beaumont? She hoped it was not the same as hers, though this gentleman did not seem the sort to seek a love potion.

When his gaze fell on Caroline, he gave the slightest flinch before smiling, a practiced expression that seemed false even at a glance. "Forgive me, I did not mean to interrupt your... business," he said, gesturing to Caroline's presence. His voice was smooth and charming, with a slight rasp that Caroline found intriguing.

"Mr. Wickham," Mr. Beaumont said, rising to his feet and extending his hand. "This is Miss Bingley, a regular customer of mine."

Caroline flushed, furious at being referred to as such. But the name Wickham caught in her mind. She had heard her brother and Mr. Darcy speak of the man in hushed tones, though they had refused to elaborate on the topic.

"Pleasure to meet you, Miss Bingley." Mr. Wickham bent in a deep bow, and Caroline's face flushed as she saw the sharp curve of his cheek and the clean line of his jaw. This business with potions and peddlers was turning her mind into a muddle. She had no business associating with a strange militia man who associated with the likes of Mr. Beaumont in acts of illicit commerce at all hours of the night. Never mind that Caroline was doing the same.

"Pray, a gentleman knows better than to interfere in a lady's business," Mr. Wickham said, taking a step towards one of the overfull shelves and kneeling with exaggerated interest to study one of the horrid bone dolls.

"Now, Miss Bingley," Mr. Beaumont said, re-corking the bottle and holding it out to Caroline. "This is an antidote," he lowered his voice as he explained. "Apply it to Mr. Darcy's skin, and it should undo the dosing, and all that will remain is the truth."

"Will it?" Finally, Mr. Beaumont had delivered some-thing useful! All thought of Mr. Wickham forgotten,

Caroline reached for the bottle, her pulse racing. "How quickly will it work?"

"Immediately." Mr. Beaumont pushed it into her palm. "But truth can be painful, Miss Bingley."

Nothing would be more painful than watching Mr. Darcy throw himself at that Bennet chit. Caroline clutched the jar tightly. Once the antidote freed Mr. Darcy from the potion's effects, he would have no reason beyond honor to follow through on the engagement. It was a good first step in ending this farce between him and Miss Elizabeth. Surely Miss Elizabeth would do something horrid before the third Sunday's reading of the banns to make herself unsuitable. Caroline was not sure what, but she could arrange something. Somehow.

"I suppose you will insist on further payment," Caroline said, wrinkling her nose.

"No need. Consider it a gift of goodwill," Mr. Beaumont said with a wry twist of his lips. "I would hate for a beautiful woman to go unsatisfied."

Caroline smiled as she tucked the antidote carefully in her reticule. "Perhaps I misjudged you, Mr. Beaumont."

The officer, Mr. Wickham, coughed. "Mr. Darcy, did you say?"

Caroline stiffened. "Why do you ask, Mr. Wickham?"

The officer chuckled, rising to his feet and sauntering towards her. "Simply curious. Mr. Darcy is an old acquaintance of mine, and I am always interested in hearing news of him." His tone was mild, but Caroline sensed a hint of danger in it. She thought of the scar on Mr. Beaumont's cheek, and her stomach tightened.

"Mr. Darcy is a friend of my brother and a guest of our home. I can tell him you inquired after him if you wish," Caroline offered, though she was not sure if she actually meant it.

"No need, Miss Bingley." Mr. Wickham smiled, but it did not reach his eyes. "We did not part on the easiest of terms, though I remember our childhood with fondness. I trust he is not ill."

"Ill?"

Mr. Wickham laughed. "Or perhaps lovesick? I heard talk of an engagement. Miss Elizabeth Bennet, was it not? We had a lively conversation. Quite a beauty, and an outspoken one at that. I admit, I had always thought Mr. Darcy the type to set his sights higher, but one can never judge another's tastes, I suppose."

Caroline gritted her teeth. "It is not his taste. Circumstances can lead a gentleman to unfortunate actions. But nothing is set as of yet."

"Ah! But the Mr. Darcy I remember is more bound by duty than desire. Even if he has no fondness for the lady, which, considering rumor, he likely does, he will not besmirch his honor by attempting to break the engagement. Not without cause."

Which was the core of Caroline's problem as well.

Mr. Wickham's smile widened, his teeth gleaming white in the lamplight. "But if something were to break his bonds of duty..."

Caroline eyed him cautiously. "What do you propose?"

Mr. Beaumont interjected, "Mr. Wickham, you were looking for a card deck, were you not? I believe I have something in stock that will suit your needs."

Mr. Wickham hesitated, his gaze moving back and

forth between Caroline and the peddler. Finally, he said, "Miss Bingley, this business might be better discussed in private." He dipped his chin towards Mr. Beaumont. "If you would excuse us?"

"As you wish." Mr. Beaumont tilted his head, and his gaze darkened. "Miss Bingley, I must remind you, truth can wound and wrong will only compound wrong."

Piffle. This peddler moralized more than a parson at Sunday services. She would not be lectured to by a man who sold potions and dolls in the dead of night. "I appreciate your concerns, Mr. Beaumont," Caroline said, forcing a smile. "But I assure you, I have the situation well in hand."

Mr. Wickham stepped towards the wagon door. The rain had eased, leaving only a heavy shroud of mist hanging over the landscape. Caroline shivered and pulled her pelisse tightly around her. When they had walked a short distance, Caroline stopped. The wagon had fallen out of sight, and the only sound was the crunch of their boots in the mud.

"Now, tell me about your proposal, Mr. Wickham."

Caroline said, tilting her chin up. "And do not play games with me. I am in no mood for more trickery."

"No trickery, Miss Bingley." Mr. Wickham said quietly. "You wish to free yourself and Mr. Darcy of the burden of Miss Elizabeth Bennet. I see this as an opportunity for us both..."

CHAPTER TEN

That night, after dinner and another round of brandy with Bingley, Darcy walked back to his rooms, pondering his next move. He did not want to bring Miss Bingley's attention to his investigation. This meant he could not simply demand her personal maid attend him in his study. That would bring gossip, and though gentry pretended not to listen to servants' gossip, most everyone did.

Worse, Margaret hardly ever seemed to leave her mistress's side. If she was not in direct attendance, she was in areas Darcy, as a gentleman of the household, could not wander into unannounced. At least, not if he wished to remain unnoticed.

He had just reached the turn to the corridor leading

to his suite when he heard soft crying. Darcy stopped and strained to hear. The sound came further ahead, in an alcove partially shielded by a thick velvet curtain. Darcy ducked behind it, his heart pounding as he caught a glimpse of a woman in a maid's cap hunched on a stool, weeping into her hands.

Darcy ventured a guess. "Margaret?"

The maid's head jerked up, and her eyes widened. Her nose was red, and her eyes swollen with tears. She held a small tin box in her hands, and Darcy could smell the sweet, acrid scent of burnt herbs.

"Sir?" the maid whispered. "Mr. Darcy?" She wiped her sleeve under her swollen eyes as she straightened her posture. "Can I help you?"

"I hope you can, Margaret. I understand you are Miss Bingley's lady's maid," Darcy began. "And last night, I overheard..." He took a breath, trying to gather his thoughts. He could sense Margaret's discomfort and said, "I understand you attempted to assist Miss Bingley with a particular matter."

"Oh, Mr. Darcy, it is lady's business, you must understand." Margaret flushed and fumbled with the tin box, shutting it abruptly and shoving it into the pocket of her apron. She folded her hands in her lap, averting her gaze.

Darcy knelt in front of her, though he knew it was highly improper. He said softly, "Margaret, I fear Miss Bingley may have involved you in something dangerous, and I only wish to ensure you are unharmed. And that no harm comes to anyone else."

"I did not do anything, sir! I swear it." Margaret twisted her apron in her hands, her face paling. "I mentioned Mr. Beaumont and how he made a sachet for my sister to draw her swain's gaze, but I did not expect Miss Bingley to seek him out. I did not know what she was planning until she had already acted, and when she insisted I help, I feared she would dismiss me. I cannot afford to lose my position, Mr. Darcy. My mother and sisters depend on me."

"Margaret, you have my word. No harm will come to you or your family." Darcy could not promise Miss Bingley would keep her post, but he would ensure Margaret had a reference and a position, even if he had to take her on at Pemberley himself. "Do you know what she purchased?"

Margaret shook her head. "Mistress said nothing of it, sir. Only that she had obtained something that would ensure her happiness. And it had something to do with you, sir." Her voice trembled, and Darcy sensed something lurking beneath her words. He was unsure if she was afraid or ashamed. Perhaps both. "That is all I can, by any means, swear to. Miss Bingley never spoke of it before, except to mutter to herself. And after..." She shook her head. "But I should never have told my mistress about Mr. Beaumont. I did not mean any harm, and if I had known Miss Bingley would do something horrid, I would never have said anything."

Darcy's thoughts raced. The maid clearly thought her mistress had done something terrible, even if she didn't know exactly what. He asked, "Margaret, will you tell me where I can find Mr. Beaumont?"

Margaret flinched. "Sir, if my mistress finds out..." she trailed off, and Darcy sensed she wanted to say more.

"Margaret, I will ensure she never knows you betrayed her confidence. But this is a matter of grave importance, and you can be instrumental in helping uncover the truth of what happened." Darcy could not believe Margaret was so blind to her mistress's machinations, but he sensed she was scared, and not entirely of Miss Bingley.

Margaret wrung her hands together, the fabric of her apron crinkling between her fingers. Finally, she let out a long breath. "Mr. Beaumont operates a traveling wagon in the forest south of Meryton. Near the old stone barn. They say he sells concoctions and potions for all sorts of ailments." She shook her head. "My sister believed her swain was charmed by one, and said Mr. Beaumont is well skilled at the trade, but I confess, I did not believe her. Anyone with eyes could see Edward, the miller's son, had been making eyes at her since last year's harvest festival."

"Mr. Beaumont. And his wagon is south of Meryton." He repeated the directions she had given. "Does he operate during the day, or only in the dark of night?"

Margaret shrugged. "I do not know. I have never met him myself. But my sister went at night, and she said he was a very odd sort. Miss Bingley as well..." The maid wrinkled her nose. "My mistress found his demeanor disconcerting, I think. Not that I would speak ill of her." She bowed her head, and Darcy sensed the tension radiating from her. "I fear she may seek Mr. Beaumont out again. She was quite upset after the Netherfield ball. Whatever she bought from him did not work as expected, and now that you and Miss Elizabeth are engaged, she has a desperate look in her eyes."

Darcy suppressed a grimace. Miss Elizabeth. He wished he knew the truth of his emotions, but the memory of her lips on his, and the fire in his veins when he held her in his arms, confused him. Was it true love or some lingering effect of the mysterious substance Miss Bingley had slipped into his drink? "I will ensure Miss Bingley does not make trouble for you or your family, Margaret," Darcy said gently. "And thank you for your honesty. I know it must have been difficult for you to reveal such things."

"Miss Elizabeth is a kind soul," Margaret said. "She and her sister. Many of the gentry do not bother to acknowledge their servants, but when she stayed, Miss Elizabeth had a smile and a kind word for everyone."

That, too, spoke well of his future bride. And Mr. Darcy noticed the maid did not speak so highly of her mistress. Darcy bowed his head and said,

"Thank you. Your information is most helpful. If you think of anything else, please do not hesitate to find me." He hesitated and added, "I will be discreet in my inquiries. I give my word."

Margaret bowed her head, and Darcy stepped away from the alcove, letting the curtain fall shut behind him. With his suspicions confirmed, he was more determined than ever to track down Mr. Beaumont and uncover the truth of what Miss Bingley had done.

It was time for answers, and Darcy would stop at nothing to find them.

CHAPTER ELEVEN

The next morning, Jane had Elizabeth come with her to Meryton to speak with Mr. Jones at his apothecary. The evening's rain had dampened the ground, and Elizabeth wrapped her shawl tighter around her shoulders as they made their way down the village's main street. By the haberdashery, she saw Miss Maria Lucas walking arm-in-arm with her mother. Jane greeted the ladies, and Lady Lucas arched an eyebrow, her gaze darting between Elizabeth and Jane with a speculative gleam in her eye.

"It seems congratulations are in order," Lady Lucas said, her tone cool. "I admit, I was shocked at how quickly you and Mr. Darcy reached an accord, especially as it is out of character for your mother to hold her tongue on such things, but your display made that accord quite plain at Netherfield."

Elizabeth's cheeks heated. Jane gave Lady Lucas a reproachful glare and said, "Mama had not wanted to share the good fortune until we settled matters."

"Quite settled," Lady Lucas said, the jealousy clear in her tone. Her daughter Maria flushed and looked away, tugging at the sleeves of her gown. "Though we must admit, it seems quite sudden. Our Charlotte was most shocked. And upset, in truth, to find herself removed from your confidence."

Elizabeth winced. Charlotte had always been a dear friend, and she had not meant to hurt her or anyone. But she could not reveal she had simply lost all her senses and dove into a scandal by kissing Mr. Darcy in full view of everyone at the Netherfield ball. To deny they were engaged to wed would remove even the pale shroud of protection Mr. Darcy's declaration offered Elizabeth's tattered reputation. "Please tell Charlotte I hope I can speak with her soon and explain it all," Elizabeth said.

"I will convey your message, but I cannot speak to how my daughter will receive it."

"Of course," Elizabeth agreed. But her stomach twisted at the thought of losing her friend entirely.

Maria Lucas bit her bottom lip as her gaze shifted between her mother and the two Bennet girls. She mumbled, "Congratulations," and Elizabeth nodded, grateful for the younger girl's attempt at tact.

"Yes! Congratulations are in order. Mr. Darcy is quite the enigma. One would have thought him overly reserved, but they say it is often the quiet ones who have the most passionate natures." Lady Lucas cocked her head, her brow furrowing. "Though one would accuse you of a love of silence, Miss Eliza."

Jane squeezed Elizabeth's hand. While Elizabeth felt terrible about her unintentional rejection of Charlotte, she did not deserve nor wish to suffer any more of Lady Lucas's poorly disguised barbs. She forced a smile and said, "One could not accuse me of silence, Lady Lucas. Fortunately, Mr. Darcy enjoys our conversation, even when we speak of silly things." Elizabeth could imagine it. Long walks and spirited discussions, with Mr. Darcy's wit and intellect a perfect match for her own.

"Silly." Lady Lucas raised a thin, graying eyebrow.

At the lady's pointed expression, Elizabeth's mood lightened, and she found herself swallowing back a laugh. "Delightful." She said, her shoulders straightening as she met Lady Lucas's gaze directly. "Nothing sillier than discussing the merits of Shakespeare and adventurous tales."

"Well." Lady Lucas sniffed.

"But we must be on to the apothecary. You know our mother and her nerves," Elizabeth said as airily as any flutterheaded dimwit. "Good day, Lady Lucas."

"And a pleasant afternoon to you both," Lady Lucas muttered, giving Jane a perfunctory nod before marching away, Maria scurrying in her wake.

When they entered the apothecary shop, Mr. Jones greeted Jane with a broad smile, his cheeks rosy and his eyes sparkling. Elizabeth studied the jars and bottles of tinctures and elixirs lining the shelves, her nose twitching at the sharp scents as Jane said, "Mr. Jones, may we ask you a question about a remedy?"

Mr. Jones brushed his greying hair from his forehead as he leaned across the counter. "Certainly, Miss Bennet, though you know nearly as much as I in the area of soothing herbs. I pray your mother's nerves have not grown worse?"

"Thankfully, no," Jane replied. "Mama is doing very well, in truth. She hardly has a megrim. Nor I, lately. And it is not a remedy, per se." She lowered her voice and said, "I know some herbs and mushrooms can have troubling effects…"

Mr. Jones peered over his glasses, his gaze shifting between Jane and Elizabeth, his face still wrinkled in confusion. "Your sisters were not out mushrooming, were they? Eating wild mushrooms can be dangerous, even when you are an experienced forager."

Jane glanced towards Elizabeth. "No, sir," Jane said, cutting Mr. Jones off. "It is a more delicate matter."

"Mushrooms?" Mr. Jones cocked his head in obvious confusion. His glasses, perched on the bridge of his nose, slid to the tip, and he adjusted them with a sheepish grin. "I hope your Miss Lydia did not make a cream of them. The fashion plates can offer strange suggestions for maintaining a lady's youth and beauty. What color is the rash?"

"No rash," Jane said hastily. "It may not be a mushroom at all. Perhaps it would be best if Lizzy explains."

"Miss Elizabeth! I heard you are soon due to wed. Tell me you did not apply some herbal concoction to your..." His gaze flitted down and back up again as he flushed. "Anywhere... intimate."

"No!" Elizabeth had thought she had reached the depths of mortification when she heard Mr. Collins threatening to defend her honor on the floor of the Netherfield ball after she'd lost herself in Mr. Darcy's kiss. But this was even more humiliating. She said, "No, nothing like that." She sighed. There was no way to speak of this gently, and every attempt she and Jane made only worsened things. "I suppose you heard about my and Mr. Darcy's kiss at Netherfield?"

Mr. Jones's cheeks flushed a brilliant red, and he swallowed visibly, his Adam's apple bobbing. "Ah, Miss Elizabeth. A gentleman should never speak of such matters," he managed, his voice strangled.

"Yes, I understand but..." Elizabeth's mouth felt dry as dust. She could not abandon the falsehood of her and Mr. Darcy's engagement even as she intimated that the gentleman's actions might have stemmed from an unknown dosing rather than desire. "While before the Netherfield ball, Mr. Darcy has been clear in his intentions towards me..." in that he had shared no intentions towards her, but Mr. Jones need not know everything, "I fear some substance introduced into his drink may have caused a temporary... addition of ardor."

Mr. Jones's expression changed from embarrassment to concern. "Gin?" he suggested, his tone gentle. "Or absinthe? A bad batch of either can cause hallucinations and loss of judgment."

"Cannot one smell or taste these?"

"Sometimes. Absinthe, in particular, is bitter and unpleasant." Mr. Jones shook his head. "Aniseed and fennel tempers the wormwood, and a sufficient amount of honey or sugar will mask the flavor, but too much absinthe can make a person ill. Or permanently muddled in the mind."

Mr. Darcy's mind had seemed clear enough yesterday morning. And he had danced well enough. A gentleman blinded by spirits would have stumbled on the dance floor or appeared unfocused and distracted. Mr. Darcy had shown none of that. Only an urgency and heat that Elizabeth found thrilling and exciting. "I do not think it was either of those things. Mr. Darcy was not overly fond of spirits. Another concoction, perhaps? Something herbal or medicinal?"

Mr. Jones sighed. "Miss Elizabeth, it is possible that Mr. Darcy was indeed dosed, though I cannot think why anyone would deliberately do such a thing."

"But if someone thought such a dose would make the gentleman more receptive to their advances?" Elizabeth suggested.

"This sounds like that potion nonsense the village gossips speak of." Mr. Jones's expression darkened. "They say a traveling peddler has set up shop in the woods south of town. He sells love potions and charms and such. Balderdash! It is all foolishness and superstition. And dangerous."

"A peddler?" Elizabeth repeated, leaning closer to Mr. Jones. She sensed Jane doing the same, her sister's skirts brushing against her own. "What peddler?"

"Mr. Beaumont, they call him. Rumors swirl about him like flies over rotten meat. The apothecaries in

London warn against such charlatans and mountebanks who sell remedies that do more harm than good. I doubt it has any connection to whatever happened at Netherfield. More likely, a surfeit of spirits and the love for a beautiful lady overtook the gentleman. It happens, sometimes."

But Elizabeth doubted Mr. Darcy had been drunk. And no taste of gin or even absinthe would have caused her to behave as she had, either. Though she was not inclined towards superstition, the potion peddler, this, Mr. Beaumont, offered the best lead she had found so far. She needed to find him, speak to him, and find out if Miss Bingley had made a purchase from his shop. But all she knew was his name and that he had a wagon south of town.

"If I wanted to speak with this Mr. Beaumont—"

"No!" Mr. Jones cut her off. "Miss Elizabeth, that man is nothing but trouble. At best, he is a fraud. At worst, he traffics in things best left alone. And even if he was genuine, dabbling in herbs and remedies without knowledge or skill can be dangerous. Why, there was an old woman near Hertford who died after imbibing an overdose of foxglove tonic. And that is just one of many examples."

Jane took Elizabeth's hand and squeezed. "Of course. We have no intention of purchasing anything from such a man, but if he is in the area, it behooves us to be aware of his presence and warn others off." Jane gave the apothecary a sweet, placating smile. "Surely you can understand that, Mr. Jones? It would be negligent if we allowed Mr. Beaumont to prey on the naïve."

Mr. Jones's expression softened. "I suppose you are right, Miss Bennet. But it is not just Mr. Beaumont I worry about. Your mother, for example. She is a dear woman, but if she sought Mr. Beaumont's help in curing her nerves or a persistent cough, it could turn deadly. Promise me, Miss Elizabeth and Miss Bennet, you will steer well clear of the man?"

Elizabeth and Jane exchanged a glance, and Jane said, "We will heed your warning, Mr. Jones. But to do so, we need to know where to avoid."

Mr. Jones hesitated before nodding. "Very well. You are both sensible young women. I trust you will exercise caution. Last I heard, he had set up his wagon in a clearing at the edge of the forest, south of the old stone barn." He sighed, rubbing his hand over his beard. "But I urge you, do not seek him out."

"Thank you, Mr. Jones. I appreciate your counsel," Elizabeth said. And she truly did. But finding this Mr. Beaumont and seeing if Miss Bingley had attempted to buy something from him could uncover the truth of what had really occurred at the Netherfield ball. Mr. Darcy deserved that much. And Elizabeth herself needed to know. Not just to see justice done, for whatever justice they could wring from such a situation, but to know if the kiss they had shared was real or the result of trickery.

She and Jane bade Mr. Jones good day and stepped outside, the damp air smelling sweet with flowers and grass as they made their way back towards Longbourn.

"A potion?" Jane asked when they were far enough away that none from the village could overhear. "It seems like something out of a fairy tale book. Or farce."

It felt to Elizabeth like something out of a farce, too. But she could not deny that something had affected Mr. Darcy at the ball. And if it was not liquor or spirits, then it was something else. A potion was as good an explanation as any. "Mr. Darcy was not drunk.

Nor was I. And they say, as often as not, there is a grain of truth in tales."

Jane nodded slowly. "Then I suppose the only solution is to find Mr. Beaumont, and learn the truth of things. But we cannot visit him alone."

"I will call on Mr. Darcy at Netherfield and share with him all I have learned," Elizabeth decided. "This concerns us both. He deserves as much as I to know the truth. Perhaps even more so."

Jane gave Elizabeth a curious glance. "Do you think there could ever be genuine affection between you and him?"

Elizabeth hesitated, remembering the kiss she and Mr. Darcy had shared, the intensity and passion of it, the way his touch made her burn. She said, "I hope there can be." If they did not marry, her reputation would be in tatters, and worse, her scandal would ruin her sisters' chances of securing suitable matches for themselves. She could not allow that to happen.

Mr. Darcy might feel nothing for her, but it was time for them to find out what Miss Bingley had done and determine the extent of the damage. Elizabeth had always valued truth and integrity over social niceties and etiquette. She would not consign them both to a lifetime of misery based on one moment of madness. She owed herself and Mr. Darcy that much.

If Mr. Darcy felt as she did, maybe they could find a way to be happy, even if it was not the arrangement society expected.

But a growing part of her hoped Mr. Darcy's feelings mirrored her growing affection for him. If there was any potential for love between them, hidden or otherwise, she would not allow it to die. She could not. Not with her heart and future happiness at stake.

Elizabeth quickened her pace as she and Jane returned home, her pulse racing. The answers waited for her with Mr. Beaumont in a wagon at the edge of the woods.

CHAPTER TWELVE

By mid-afternoon, Darcy had grown thoroughly sick of Miss Caroline Bingley. She seemed to be everywhere, hovering at the edges of conversations between Darcy and Bingley, and chattering inanely about the weather and the latest fashions from London. She followed Darcy to the stables, insisting that they ride together, which gave him no chance to search for Mr. Beaumont's wagon in the light of day. Finally, returning his horse to the stable, Darcy lost his patience and said, "Miss Bingley, you are a lovely young lady, but if you continue to follow me like a pet spaniel, I shall be forced to lose my temper."

Miss Bingley flushed crimson, her lips trembling as

she sputtered, "I assure you, Mr. Darcy, I meant no offense." Her eyes widened, and she added, "It is only that we are friends, you and I, are we not? I thought perhaps I could offer you a sympathetic ear in your betrothal difficulties."

As the lady in question was the most likely culprit of his "betrothal difficulties," Darcy had a difficult time maintaining his composure. He said, "Miss Bingley, you know as well as I that Miss Elizabeth and I are engaged by mutual choice. Please do not pretend you are unaware."

"Of course! It was all just so sudden. Surely, the effects—" Miss Bingley fell into a fit of coughing, one that to Darcy's eyes seemed contrived, but he did not remark on it. "That is, I wish you both the happiest of unions. But I wonder..." Her gaze darted towards the distant trees, and her tone changed abruptly, turning teasing. "What it was like. Your kiss. With Miss Elizabeth." She giggled, and Darcy blinked, unsure of how to respond.

"Miss Bingley, I suspect you know perfectly well how kisses are managed," he said stiffly. "And if not, it is still indecent to ask."

"My apologies!" Miss Bingley demurred, pressing her hands to her lips. She blinked, eyes shining, and Darcy feared she might cry. But would even tears be an act? He could not know. "I only meant..." She paused, taking a breath. "Forgive me, Mr. Darcy. I can be silly sometimes. A flutterhead, as my mother would say when I was a girl. Before she passed..." She swallowed, and Darcy, despite his suspicion of her motives, sensed a genuine sadness in her tone. He should not pity Miss Bingley, not when her actions had likely caused his present distress. But he could not entirely ignore her pain.

"It is difficult for a child to lose her mother." It had been difficult for him. His sister too, though Georgiana had been barely six years of age when the fever claimed their mother. Darcy remembered the grief and isolation he had felt, his father's grief seeming to drive them apart, leaving Darcy feeling isolated and alone. And Georgiana, even as a little girl, had clung to him with all her strength, crying, "Mama!" at her mother's bedroom door, tiny fists curling into the fabric of his coat. "Especially for a daughter," he added.

Miss Bingley looked up, her eyes still bright with unshed tears. "My mother was not always the easiest woman. She expected a lot of my sister and I. But she loved us, and I miss her dearly." She shook her head, blinking rapidly and pasting a smile on her lips. "Enough of my sentimentality! Mr. Darcy, I must apologize for following you like this. I suppose I am still adjusting to the idea of you being married, especially to a lady from such a humble family." Miss Bingley wrinkled her nose. "But I am sure your choice speaks volumes about your character, if you are certain of your feelings for her."

Darcy was far from certain of his feelings for Miss Elizabeth, another problem he could lie at Miss Bingley's feet. But he had no intention of allowing Miss Bingley to manipulate him into admitting to uncertainty or ambivalence. He said, "I assure you, Miss Bingley, my affections for Miss Elizabeth are as steadfast as my honor." He spoke the words with conviction, knowing that even if Miss Bingley had tricked him into a passionate embrace with Miss Elizabeth, he would not allow her to spread rumors about a lack of commitment on his part.

Mr. Darcy did not have time to ponder Miss Bingley's reaction to his statement because a footman approached, his uniform pressed and his boots polished to a high shine. His dark hair curled over his brow, and his green eyes were earnest as he said, "Sir, Miss Elizabeth Bennet has come to call. She awaits you in the parlor."

Miss Bingley pursed her lips, but Darcy ignored her, bowing to her hastily and saying, "Excuse me, Miss Bingley."

Miss Bingley's lips tightened, her blue eyes hardening as she glared at the footman. The expression passed in heartbeats, the lady quickly schooling her features back to a cool, neutral facade.

If Darcy had doubted Miss Bingley's hatred of Miss Elizabeth, or her belief that Darcy belonged with Miss Bingley instead of his future bride, her reaction now convinced him. And Margaret's information, combined with his inability to search for Mr. Beaumont's wagon without Miss Bingley's interference, only strengthened Darcy's determination to uncover the truth of the potion.

As he strode away from Miss Bingley towards the house, Darcy felt Miss Bingley's gaze burning into his back. But he could not focus on her machinations now. His priority remained Miss Elizabeth and, to his surprise, he looked forward to speaking with her about more than what he had learned about the potion from the maid. He simply wanted to spend time with her. To hear her talk about literature and philosophy, her observations and opinions. He wanted to laugh and tease and even share another kiss, as brief and unexpected as the first.

And that alone was enough to disturb him.

Could a love potion, if such a thing existed, create feelings where none had existed before? Or was it only a catalyst for desire that already lay buried beneath the surface?

Darcy wished he knew, but he would not settle for half-truths and fancies.

When he reached the parlor, Miss Elizabeth stood waiting, her cheeks flushed from the wind, a riot of brown curls framing her face. She smiled when she saw him, and Darcy's pulse quickened. "Miss Elizabeth. What brings you here today?"

"I have news," Miss Elizabeth said. "Pertaining to our mutual concern." She glanced at the half-open door and said, "Perhaps it would be best if we take a walk? Together? Outside?"

'Where none could overhear' hung in the air, unspoken.

Darcy agreed, and soon they were strolling arm-in-arm through the gardens towards a secluded path winding through the surrounding countryside. The twin tensions of desire and secrets hummed under their silence. To say that he had questioned Miss Bingley's maid, who had claimed Miss Bingley had gone to a peddler and somehow acquired a potion, and worse, that it had worked, seemed too foolish to speak aloud.

The ridiculousness of it was why Darcy had planned to investigate it before involving his future wife. But now that Miss Elizabeth was here, he could not, in conscience, keep it from her.

As they walked, she worried at her lower lip with her teeth, glancing at him with an unreadable expression. Finally, when they were a distance from the estate, she stopped, turning to face him. "I fear what I have to say might sound incredible," she began.

Darcy laughed. "Not as unbelievable as what I have uncovered."

Miss Elizabeth's eyes widened, and she said, "What

have you learned?" Her head cocked. "Pray it does not have to do with peddlers and potions."

Darcy gaped at her. "Miss Bingley's maid told me of a peddler named Mr. Beaumont, who is selling concoctions to cure heartache and seduce reluctant swains." Darcy could not help but add, "How did you—?"

"Mr. Jones, the apothecary, was near apoplexy when he warned us away from the man. Dangerous charlatan was what he called him." Miss Elizabeth lifted an eyebrow, her lips quirking upwards. "But considering our situation, I thought it was worth looking into. He goes by—"

"Mr. Beaumont, I know. After some persuasion, Miss Bingley's maid revealed her mistress had sought the man out." Darcy ran a hand through his hair, tugging at the strands. "Miss Elizabeth, I fear what has transpired between us is Miss Bingley's work, or at least something she attempted."

Elizabeth sighed. "I suspect so, though we will not know for certain until we confront the man."

"I had planned to call on him today. Though I am given to understand he only conducts business in the evening, I hoped he might make an exception for a gentleman with deep pockets." Darcy flushed, realizing how callous he sounded.

"Then we shall confront him this evening," Elizabeth said.

"No," Darcy protested. "I cannot permit you to place yourself in danger, Miss Elizabeth."

Elizabeth snorted. "Miss Bingley and half of the village seem to have called on this Mr. Beaumont, and none are gone missing or mysteriously slain. The danger is in his products, not in facing the man directly." She placed her hand on his chest, her palm warm even through his waistcoat. "And if we are to make a future together and not a mockery, whatever we decide to do, it is best we do it together."

Darcy felt a surge of desire, stronger than what had driven him to kiss Miss Elizabeth at the ball. Not just desire for her body, but admiration of her courage, her wit, and her determination. "Together," he agreed, his pulse hammering as he stared down into her brown eyes.

If this connection he felt to her came from Miss

Bingley's potion, he had no wish to fight it. Darcy took a step towards her. "May I kiss you?" he asked.

Miss Elizabeth's lips parted, her breath coming quicker. "Yes." She met his gaze, and Darcy felt a jolt of awareness as their lips met, his hands settling on her waist. He kissed her slowly, savoring the sweetness of her mouth and the scent of lavender in her hair. She tilted her head, her arms looping around his neck as she tugged him closer. She pressed against him, warm and right in his arms. Darcy's desire flared, his blood heating as he deepened the kiss, their tongues tangling.

If this was true, he wanted nothing more than to lay her on the grass beneath them and show her what she meant to him, desire and beyond.

But if it was false...?

Sanity intruded, and Darcy reluctantly pulled away, his breathing ragged. Miss Elizabeth's cheeks were flushed, her gaze locked with his.

"Tonight," he said. "You will stay for dinner, and then I will see you home in Bingley's carriage. If we make a stop to meet Mr. Beaumont..."

"Together then," Elizabeth repeated, brushing a stray curl from her forehead. "While I regret the circumstances, I am glad we are united in this."

Darcy held out his arm, and she took it, resting her hand on the crook of his elbow as they made their way back towards Netherfield, towards what could be a reckoning or a revelation.

CHAPTER THIRTEEN

During the final course of what had been an awkward and unsatisfying meal which only Mr. Hurst seemed to relish, Miss Bingley, glaring daggers at Elizabeth, tapped her spoon down on the edge of her plate and said, "I think I shall excuse myself early and retire." She turned to her sister. "Louisa?"

Miss Hurst shrugged, draining the last of her wine. "I am not tired yet, Caroline. But please, do not linger on my account. I am used to your fits and starts."

Miss Bingley flushed. "Very well, then. Mr. Darcy, Miss Elizabeth, it was a delight." Her tone dripped sarcasm, and Elizabeth refused to look away or let the lady's scorn cow her.

"Likewise," Elizabeth said, taking a bite of her syllabub. The sweet custard coated her tongue, and she smiled, licking a bit of cream from her bottom lip. She noted Mr. Darcy's gaze shifting to her lips. His pupils dilated, and Elizabeth suppressed a shiver. Miss Bingley sniffed, gathering her skirts and rising, and Elizabeth watched her depart with mixed relief and unease.

Flustered at his sister's behavior, Mr. Bingley cleared his throat. "She is acting rather oddly tonight. Do you think...?" He trailed off, and Mrs. Hurst shrugged, and her husband let out a long belch.

Mrs. Hurst shot her husband an irritated glare. "Really, Thomas? We have guests."

"Darcy is practically family, and that makes Miss Elizabeth near the same," Mr. Hurst said, unruffled by his wife's ire. He scooped up a spoonful of syllabub, winking at Darcy as he swallowed.

Mr. Bingley coughed and rubbed his hand over the back of his neck. "It grows late. Darcy?"

Mr. Darcy leaned towards Elizabeth and whispered, "Shall we make our excuses?"

Elizabeth nodded, and Mr. Darcy said, "Bingley, if you do not mind my making use of the carriage, I will see Miss Elizabeth returned to Longbourn."

Mr. Bingley turned to his sister. "Louisa, will you chaperone?"

Elizabeth stifled a groan. Of all the things to ruin their plans to find Mr. Beaumont, being forced by propriety to have Miss Bingley's sister join them was not something Elizabeth had expected.

Mrs. Hurst's nose wrinkled in displeasure, and her lips flattened into a thin line as she glanced at her husband, who yawned and said, "I do not see the point of dragging my wife out at this hour. Short of driving the carriage straight to the vicarage and tumbling each other in the pews, there is not much Darcy and Miss Elizabeth can do to worsen the current damage to their reputations."

Mr. Bingley sputtered, and Elizabeth stared, unsure whether to laugh or sink under the table in mortification.

"Thomas!" Mrs. Hurst protested, but there was little heat in it.

"Come now," Mr. Hurst said, "it is just a small jest. Amongst near family. And in less than three weeks, you will be husband and wife. Louisa and I certainly went on a few carriage rides before we took our vows." He winked, and Mrs. Hurst blushed scarlet.

"Be—. Be that as it may," Mr. Bingley said, still stammering, "perhaps Darcy and Miss Elizabeth prefer to... umm...."

"I will, on my honor, see Miss Elizabeth home safely, with her virtue intact."

"Good enough for me," Mr. Hurst said with another expansive shrug. "Come along, Louisa. Your sister is right. It is late, and we would all do well to rest."

Mrs. Hurst rose, casting a sidelong glance at her husband but did not argue as they left, leaving Mr. Bingley and Elizabeth alone with Mr. Darcy.

"I suppose it is settled then," Mr. Bingley said, somewhat hesitantly. "Unless Miss Elizabeth objects?"

"Not at all," Elizabeth replied, her pulse fluttering

with anticipation and not a small amount of dread. What if Mr. Beaumont was only an ordinary peddler, and Miss Bingley had purchased nothing but a useless mix of spirits and kitchen herbs? It seemed more likely than an actual love potion. And as crassly as Mr. Hurst had phrased it, Elizabeth's reputation would not be further compromised by sharing a carriage with Mr. Darcy. It was unlikely they would or even could commit a greater act of brazen impropriety than they had already engaged in at the Netherfield ball.

Mr. Darcy cleared his throat. "Excellent. Shall we?" He offered his arm, and Elizabeth took it, Mr. Beaumont forgotten for a heartbeat as she studied Mr. Darcy's handsome profile.

Mr. Bingley sent a footman ahead to prepare the carriage, a sleek, dark vehicle with dangling lamps, and after Mr. Bingley saw the pair off, Elizabeth and Mr. Darcy informed the driver of their planned destination and they set out. The night air was crisp and damp, and Elizabeth snuggled deeper into her shawl, leaning against Mr. Darcy's shoulder. He rested his hand over hers, his touch sending a rush of warmth through her skin.

"Mr. Hurst is certainly unconventional," Elizabeth finally ventured.

Mr. Darcy shook his head and said, "I cannot say I appreciated his wit. Not at your expense."

Elizabeth murmured, "No. But he is not incorrect, in some ways. Our situation is unfortunate, but it could be worse. And soon we will know the truth of things, and we can move forward accordingly."

Mr. Darcy tensed beside her. "Miss Elizabeth, I do not intend to leave you disgraced or cast aside. Whatever we uncover, I have committed to this engagement. I will not renege on my pledge to you. My honor demands such."

His tone was firm, and Elizabeth was grateful for his steadfastness, even as she feared a life formed in honor and duty rather than genuine affection. But if their current ease was due solely to the effects of the potion, then she had little to hope for more. She said, "Thank you, Mr. Darcy. Your reassurance eases some of my anxiety." She hesitated, drawing a breath. "Have you considered what you will do when we learn the truth?"

Mr. Darcy's silence stretched long enough that Elizabeth thought he might not answer. Then he said, "Miss Bingley must face consequences for what she has done." He exhaled heavily. "Beyond her daft scheme to force my affections through sorcery, the results could have been far worse even than our current predicament. She could have poisoned me, for example. And she may yet poison someone else."

"True," Elizabeth thought back to what Mr. Jones had said about the dangers of dabbling in herbs without knowledge or skill and shivered. If Mr. Darcy had been hurt or killed, Elizabeth could not bear the thought. Though the circumstances of their engagement had been forced upon them, she found she genuinely cared for the gentleman. His initial pride and haughtiness had faded in the wake of his recent displays of honor and kindness towards her.

"Though I cannot imagine how she can be punished for purchasing a concoction of herbs from a peddler," Mr. Darcy said, frustration coloring his tone. "There is no law against foolishness or even mischief. And Bingley dotes on his sister. His loyalty is his greatest strength and fault. I could not ask him to choose between us."

Elizabeth patted Mr. Darcy's hand, admiring its long,

elegant fingers in the darkness. "Perhaps not. But if Miss Bingley's goal was to secure your regard, she has surely failed. Perhaps that will be enough to stop her from taking such drastic measures again." It was not enough, but it would have to suffice. "And it is better to know the truth for ourselves, so we can determine the best course of action."

"I hope it is enough." Mr. Darcy frowned, his gaze focused on the curtain fluttering over the window, his expression inscrutable.

The carriage jolted over a rut, and Elizabeth nearly tumbled into Mr. Darcy's lap, her breath coming in a gasp. He caught her, holding her steady with one powerful arm wrapped around her waist. Elizabeth's pulse pounded as she glanced up into his dark eyes, so close to her own. She wondered if he would kiss her again. Mr. Hurst's words echoed in her mind, and she swallowed, suddenly wondering what illicit activities, short of disgrace, one could engage in inside a carriage.

But Mr. Darcy gently steadied her and helped her sit back against the cushioned seat. "Are you well, Miss Elizabeth?"

"Quite well," Elizabeth said, her face hot with embarrassment. She glanced out the window, recognizing the familiar dark woodlands that marked the outskirts of Meryton. They were close to Mr. Beaumont's supposed location now.

Elizabeth took a shaky breath. She could not allow herself to be distracted by her desires for Mr. Darcy, whatever their cause. They had a task to accomplish. And Elizabeth intended to see it done.

Soon, the carriage rumbled to a stop, and a footman hopped down, opening the door and lowering a lantern to light their way. "The road is too narrow for the carriage. You will need to go on foot from here," he explained.

"Thank you," Mr. Darcy said. "Stay with the carriage. We will not be long."

The footman inclined his head in a half bow as he stepped back, and Mr. Darcy climbed out, turning back to offer his hand to Elizabeth. Elizabeth had half expected him to insist she stay behind, and she was glad he had made no such effort. She took his hand, slipping out onto the packed earth, inhaling the damp, loamy scent of the surrounding woods.

Mr. Darcy adjusted the collar of his greatcoat against the chill breeze, and Elizabeth did the same, huddling into the wool of her shawl as the footman handed Mr. Darcy the lantern. He and Elizabeth set off down the path, the steady lantern light illuminating the rough dirt track before them.

They walked in silence, listening for any sound of Mr. Beaumont's wagon or other signs of his presence.

As Elizabeth and Darcy made their way, a growing mist enveloped them, tickling the hairs on her nape and the back of her wrists. She tasted it, cool and brackish on her tongue, and touched the hem of her dress, feeling the dampness of the fabric clinging to her legs. The air smelled sour, like rotting leaves and fetid water, and she heard rustling in the trees, the snapping of twigs and the crunch of acorns underfoot.

Elizabeth exchanged a nervous glance with Darcy, whose jaw tightened as he gripped the lantern handle.

"That is the barn, I think," Elizabeth said, pointing through the gloom to a dark shape hunkering low over the path. The structure seemed ancient and abandoned, the stone walls covered in moss and creeping vines. A wooden door swung on rusty hinges, creaking in the breeze. "The wagon should be nearby."

They walked, Elizabeth shifting closer to Mr. Darcy, grateful for his solid presence at her side. The trees thinned even as the mist thickened, shrouding the ground in a wet, cold veil. She felt it beading on her eyelashes and coating her cheeks like tears. After another five minutes or so walking, she spotted a clearing, but no wagon waited there.

"He cannot have moved on already?" Elizabeth asked, disappointment curdling in her stomach. Perhaps she had misunderstood Mr. Jones's directions?

Mr. Darcy led her further into the clearing. He pointed at the ground, where wheel marks could still be seen, ruts in the muddy earth, and a pile of leaves and broken sticks near one tree. "Something was parked here, and for some time, judging by the depth of these ruts. And this littering suggests the clearing has not been empty for long." Mr. Darcy gestured to a clump of crushed grass. "It's raked over.

There is no reason to drag a wagon through a wood unless it is used to set up shop. And where else could that be? We are south of the old barn, as both Mr. Jones and Miss Margaret instructed."

Elizabeth nodded, stepping over a fallen log. Her slippers squelched in the mud, and she wrinkled her nose at the stink of animal waste and decomposition. "But if Mr. Beaumont is not here, then what do we do?"

Mr. Darcy paced, the lantern swinging wildly in his grasp and lighting his face in flickering shadows. "We can circle the clearing and check the woods. Perhaps Mr. Beaumont just moves his wagon around?" He grimaced, his features tightening in frustration. "This cannot be for nothing."

"Do you hear that?" Elizabeth asked, tilting her head towards the trees. She heard a rustling, and Darcy froze, turning towards the sound.

The mist swirled, thick and opaque, and Elizabeth saw a shadow moving within it. She heard the muffled crunch of leaves as the shadowed figure advanced. Fear clogged her throat. Her heart raced, blood roaring through her ears.

Mr. Darcy called out, "Who goes there? Show yourself."

A voice called out, "Hallooo!"

Elizabeth recognized a hunched figure in a long, ragged cloak. A pale, gnarled fist thrust from the figure's too short sleeves, grasping a long staff. "Tell me you are not here for that defalcator. A cheat and liar is the so called Mr. Beaumont."

"You know him?" Elizabeth asked, hopeful.

"Aye," the old man cackled. The hood of his cloak obscured his features, though a tuft of gray beard stuck out below his chin. "He is well known around here. Potions and empty promises, he sells." He tapped his staff twice on the ground to emphasize his point. "Never trust a peddler, I say. No matter his wares."

"We need to speak with him," Elizabeth insisted. "We are..." She glanced at Darcy.

"On the matter of a love potion," Mr. Darcy said.

"Love potion!" The old man threw back his head and laughed, revealing a smattering of uneven teeth with large, dark gaps between. The movement disturbed his hood. Dirt smudged his pale face, and Elizabeth glimpsed a silvery scar running over his cheek. "Is that what old Beaumont told you?" he asked.

"He told us nothing," Mr. Darcy interrupted, irritation edging his tone. He drew himself up to his full height, his broad shoulders and stern features imposing even in the growing mist. "We merely need to ascertain a purchase he made at a lady's behest."

"How long did your lady spend over the basin, emptying her guts?"

"Not me!" Elizabeth protested. "Nor Mr. Darcy. Another lady, not us. Miss Bingley, perhaps you have heard of her?"

"I do not make a hobby of conversing with my betters," the old man said. "But if this lady is ill, you would do better to consult an apothecary than this fraud. Beaumont sells fool's hopes and dreams, and those who buy them are fools too." He spat, his phlegm striking a nearby rock. "You waste your time."

Darcy's posture tensed, and Elizabeth could sense his anger growing. "Still, we would like to speak with him. Do you know, sir, where he has moved his wares?"

"Sir!" The old man laughed again. "No sir for me. Only a wandering soul in search of honest coin." He waved his stick, and Elizabeth saw it was topped with a carved bird skull, bleached white and gleaming. "But if it is Beaumont you seek, the nearest town, not far from here, is Meryton. He is likely drinking away his ill-gotten gains in the tavern. That is his way."

Elizabeth's head felt overfull. If her and Mr. Darcy's kiss was not the result of a love potion, then what had caused it?

Mr. Darcy pulled his arm from hers as he reached into his greatcoat. "If I were to offer this honest coin," he said, his tone dripping sarcasm, "would it persuade you to tell us more?" He tossed a silver coin, and the old man snatched it out of the air.

"Mr. Beaumont is fond of ale and spirits and the ladies who serve them," the old man said, rubbing the coin between his fingers. "He also likes to make strange figures from bones. He spends hours fitting them together from bits and pieces from animals he finds dead in the woods."

Elizabeth shivered, and the old man chuckled. "Strange, yes. But no stranger than the costumes he puts on them." He glanced down at the coin. "If you want my advice, forget about Beaumont and his concoctions." He ran a thumb over the skull atop his stick, his eyes seeming almost to glitter in the light of Mr. Darcy's lantern. "They do no better than to reveal what is already truth."

Elizabeth glanced at Mr. Darcy, her thoughts racing. How could they trust this man who claimed to know Mr. Beaumont, but spoke in riddles that made no sense? They could not, not entirely. But despite his strangeness, Elizabeth thought she sensed no malice in the man.

An owl screeched in the distance. Leaning on his stick, the old man folded himself into an awkward bow. "Your pardon, good people. I have lingered too long, and it grows late. Love is a strange thing. No potion or poultice can create love from nothing, no matter what Beaumont claims. Take care and fare thee well." Leaning heavily on his stick, he started across the clearing, his stick tap-tapping as he disappeared into the mist.

Elizabeth waited until the sound of the old man's movements faded into silence and then said, "What an odd fellow."

"Odd is a mild word for it," Mr. Darcy said, frowning. "I wonder if he knows Mr. Beaumont at all."

"If what he said is true... then maybe our kiss was caused by something else." Maybe it had come from true passion?

"Perhaps," Mr. Darcy said, but his tone held doubt. He shook his head and offered his arm to Elizabeth. "Either way, we will learn nothing more here. Let us return to Bingley's carriage. I said I would see you home safely, and I shall."

Elizabeth nodded and again tucked her hand in the crook of his arm. As they made their way back through the woods, the mist seemed to clear, and breaks formed in the heavy cloud cover above, revealing stars and a slice of moon. Without the hope of finding Mr. Beaumont and setting things straight, Elizabeth felt something inside her shift. She and Mr. Darcy would be married in less than three weeks. Even so, she barely knew him, beyond what their shared kiss had revealed.

As they approached Mr. Bingley's carriage, the footman scrambled to open the door, and Elizabeth sank into the velvet seats, Mr. Darcy beside her. She wanted to ask him what he thought, to discuss the old man's cryptic words and their future. But though Mr. Darcy sat beside her, close enough to feel the heat of his hip pressed at her side, he remained silent, lost in his thoughts. Elizabeth did not push. For once, words escaped her.

The carriage lurched forward, and Elizabeth gazed out the window, watching the passing woods and fields fade into darkness, leaving behind only questions and doubts.

CHAPTER FOURTEEN

Lady Catherine de Bourgh was a staunch believer in the art of posture and the necessity of a fine kedgeree in the morning. Curried eggs were masterful for the digestion, and Lady Catherine prided herself on fine digestion nearly as much as she prided herself on maintaining a trim figure despite her advancing age. She was just finishing her last mouthful when a footman entered the room and, with a bow, announced, "Mr. Collins is here to see you, madam. He seems... agitated."

How had Mr. Collins returned to Hunsford so soon? Lady Catherine frowned. And agitated? Well, Mr. Collins was often agitated. Had he persuaded one of his cousins to accept his proposal already? The gentleman had done better for himself than she had expected. Lady Catherine supposed she would have to endure her parson and protege's youthful enthusing over his future bride, whoever of that gaggle of Bennet girls she might be.

"Show Mr. Collins in," she ordered with a nod.

Bowing again, the footman withdrew. Lady Catherine placed her fork delicately on the edge of her plate and took a sip of her chocolate, savoring the rich bitterness on her tongue. Some sweetened their chocolate, but Lady Catherine found the bitterness enhanced the flavor.

Lady Catherine had barely taken a second sip when Mr. Collins burst into the breakfast room with a flourish of his coat, his hair standing on end and his eyes wide. He did not look the sort of agitated of a gentleman bearing good tidings, and his next words confirmed her suspicions. "My dear patroness! I came from Hertfordshire at once! There is terrible, terrible news." He tugged at his cravat, which appeared hastily tied and stained with perspiration. "I must apologize for disturbing your breakfast, but it cannot wait! Why when I think of what has transpired, it is enough to bring on palpitations! Palpitations, I say!"

Lady Catherine leaned back in her chair, fixing Mr. Collins with a stare that had intimidated greater men into quaking silence. "Sit, Mr. Collins. Tell me what distresses you so."

Mr. Collins dropped into the seat across from her, his face ashen. "It is Mr. Darcy, Lady Catherine! Your esteemed nephew. He has done something... unspeakable! A scandal, to be sure!"

"Fitzwilliam?" Her nephew was hardly the sort to involve himself in scandals. Lady Catherine sniffed, dabbing at her lips with her napkin. "What nonsense is this?" Though Mr. Collins possessed the laudable good sense that came from listening to her sensible advice, he was also prone to exaggeration and flights of fancy. "What scandal could he have involved himself in?"

Mr. Collins clutched at his chest. "It is horrible, Lady Catherine! Simply horrible! Mr. Darcy..." He swallowed, his Adam's apple bobbing. "Mr. Darcy..."

Lady Catherine's temper flared. "Mr. Darcy what?" She thumped her walking stick against the floor.

Mr. Collins jumped and then sputtered, "Mr. Darcy —at Netherfield— he kissed my cousin, Miss Elizabeth Bennet." His expression turned sour. "Right there at the Netherfield ball, in front of everyone. It was indecent, shocking! The banns are not yet read, and Mr. Darcy claims they are already engaged."

Lady Catherine stared at her parson in disbelief. This was preposterous. Fitzwilliam engaging in such a display was beyond imagining. "Surely, Mr. Collins, there is some mistake." Her horror at Mr. Collins' revelation was growing. What about Anne's future? Her nephew might not have been overly solicitous towards Lady Catherine's daughter, but surely, he would have offered some explanation before casting Anne aside? "My nephew is an honorable gentleman, and he would not behave in such a way!" She raised a finger to emphasize her point.

"That is precisely what I thought," Mr. Collins said. "But what could I do? What could anyone do? Miss Elizabeth and Mr. Darcy, they were utterly shameless, right in the ballroom. Right there for all to see!"

His voice rose to a whine, and Lady Catherine winced.

"And you traveled from Hertfordshire immediately?" Lady Catherine asked, her mind whirling.

"As soon as the carriage could be prepared! I did not want you to be taken unaware, Lady Catherine."

Lady Catherine scowled. This had taken her quite unawares, though to be fair, as much as she wanted to pound someone with her cane until they bled, she could not in good conscience beat her parson for his haste to bring her such appalling news. Nor could she doubt Mr. Collins sincerity.

At the same time, Mr. Collins sometimes tended towards exaggeration. It was a point of character Lady Catherine had tried, and failed, to train out of him. Perhaps this was all a misunderstanding. Fitzwilliam was many things, but promiscuous or vulgar, he was not. "How fortunate you did so," she said, trying to keep her tone calm.

If it was not a misunderstanding, then this Elizabeth Bennet must have forced herself on Fitzwilliam, somehow. Young men often thought more with their lower heads than the upper ones. Lady Catherine had used such tendencies to her advantage while in the flush of youth. She thought her nephew possessed greater strength of character, but apparently not. And of course, it would again be up to Lady Catherine to remedy the situation. Sooner rather than later, it seemed.

Mr. Collins wrung his hands. "I confess, Lady Catherine, I did not know what else to do."

"You did well to come to me, Mr. Collins." Lady Catherine rose, folding her napkin with deliberate care. "We will depart for Netherfield as soon as my luggage is readied."

Mr. Collins might exaggerate, but not by this much. Something was amiss, and Lady Catherine resolved to find out what had transpired and guarantee the restoration of Fitzwilliam's reputation and the family's good name. And if that meant confronting a brazen miss who sought to seduce her nephew into marriage by any means necessary, so be it. Lady Catherine had faced down greater foes. She would prevail.

She patted Mr. Collins's arm, and he flinched. "Do not fear, my good parson. We will make this right."

Mr. Collins sighed with evident relief. "You are most understanding, Lady Catherine."

"Indeed, I am." She tapped her stick against the floor. She would spare no effort to find the truth. And if Miss Elizabeth Bennet had indeed played Fitzwilliam false, the lady would pay dearly for it.

CHAPTER FIFTEEN

Netherfield's parlor seemed overfull as it strained to contain all seven Bennets, Darcy, Bingley, and both of his sisters. Mr. Hurst alone opted to entertain himself elsewhere, which, judging by the smell of brandy on his breath when Darcy had passed him in the corridor, had already involved a glass or two of Bingley's finest. Though no rain had yet fallen, the afternoon sky was heavy with the promise of it. Cool, damp air blew in through the fluttering curtains, and Darcy struggled not to fidget as the parlor grew increasingly warm in the stuffy manner of such spaces.

Given his head, Darcy would rather have taken Miss Elizabeth out for another carriage ride or a healthy walk through Netherfield's grounds. But the promise of rain and the hour of their arrival had conspired to keep the group indoors.

Miss Elizabeth sat at Darcy's side, her index finger tapping at the side of her teacup in an unconscious gesture that Darcy found strangely alluring. She appeared more tired than ill at ease, something Darcy understood, having awakened too early with the words of the old man from the previous night echoing in through his dreams. "No potion or poultice can create love from nothing..."

The group sat in a rough circle on three more armchairs and a pair of sofas with Mrs. Bennet across from Miss Elizabeth, and Mr. Bennet between his wife and Miss Bingley. On Miss Bingley's opposite side sat Mrs. Hurst and then Darcy. Miss Elizabeth was on Darcy's left, and from there was a sofa with her three youngest sisters. Miss Lydia, barely months older than Darcy's own sister but with a demeanor that was both more outgoing and less mannered, leaned forward on her chair, a plate with a half-eaten tart balanced on her knee. Miss Kitty sat beside her, occasionally coughing into a handkerchief. Miss Mary, the plainest of the lot, stared down at her hands, her eyelids half-shut and her hands clasped in her lap. Sometimes her lips moved, as if she was engaging in a silent monologue or prayer. Miss Bennet sat in an armchair beside Bingley, who stole glances at the lady more often than strictly within the bounds of propriety.

Darcy, who had been glancing at Miss Elizabeth in much the same manner, could find no room for fault, as much as he wished to, if only to berate himself. It was not wrong to admire one's future wife. And if what the beggar had said was true, he need not doubt his admiration.

Except, the entire thing had been so sudden. Could these feelings truly be natural?

"Mr. Darcy," Mrs. Bennet interrupted his thoughts. "You do not eat, and there is plenty for everyone. Take another one." She pointed her fan at the tray, where a scattering of several delicate sandwiches, tarts, and sweetmeats lay arranged. Miss Lydia and Miss Kitty had devoured at least half and were nibbling at another pair while Miss Mary watched, her fingers twitching.

Darcy forced a smile and picked up a sandwich, which he placed on a plate beside his teacup with a muttered "thank you." Miss Elizabeth's lips twitched, her tired eyes for a moment lighting with mirth, and he felt a surge of warmth towards the lady that he could not deny. Did not want to deny.

"It is I who should thank you!" Mrs. Bennet waved her hand in a sweeping motion that encompassed Darcy, the tray, and the entire table. "This tea is delightful! And these tarts! Your cook is truly talented, Mr. Bingley!"

Miss Bingley cut in, her voice soft and surprisingly sweet, "We are fortunate to have brought a skilled cook with us from London. She is worth her weight in gold, as you can see." She smiled. "I believe Miss Eliza has also enjoyed our tarts. We can have our cook send along the recipe, if you like."

"That would be lovely!" Mrs. Bennet beamed.

"Oh, it is nothing." Miss Bingley demurred, her gaze moving to Darcy.

Darcy shifted, feeling uncomfortable. Miss Bingley had been solicitous towards Elizabeth and her family since their arrival. He should have been relieved, but he found himself wary of Miss Bingley's sudden change in demeanor.

Mrs. Bennet, who was by far the most enamored of fruit tarts, moved another two onto her plate. "It is a delight to find our families growing so much closer. Mr. Bingley, I do hope you are enjoying our company as much as we are enjoying yours!" She patted his hand, and Bingley, whose attention remained focused on Jane Bennet, blinked and offered her a distracted smile.

Miss Bingley nodded, her eyes bright with a good humor Darcy had not seen in her since before his kiss with Miss Elizabeth at the Netherfield ball. She took a breath, and Darcy braced for whatever clever compliment or veiled insult she might deliver next.

But Miss Bingley said, "It shames me to admit, but I owe both Miss Elizabeth and Mr. Darcy an apology."

Darcy stiffened, his grip tightening around his teacup. Miss Bingley was not the sort who easily admitted wrongdoing. For a mad moment, he wondered if she would admit to doctoring his drink with a possibly fraudulent potion, but he dismissed the idea. Miss Bingley had no reason to admit to such a thing. And despite her change in attitude, he could not bring himself to trust her.

Miss Bingley continued, her gaze lowered in apparent contrition, "My behavior at the Netherfield ball, both towards Miss Elizabeth and Mr. Darcy, has been inappropriate and unforgivable. I have allowed pride and," She flicked her fan open, using it to cover her mouth as she let out a nervous chuckle, "perhaps a touch of jealousy to interfere with my good manners and conduct. I have always been fond of Mr. Darcy and hoped..." she trailed off, shaking her head. "It matters not. Mr. Darcy's affection for Miss Elizabeth is obvious, and I am happy for them both."

Only through years of managing his expression beneath the weight of his father's lectures did Darcy manage not to gape. Elizabeth breathed in sharply through her teeth.

Mrs. Bennet exclaimed, "My dear Miss Bingley, that is a heartfelt apology indeed! I have not seen such an admirable speech in ages." She paused, her gaze flickering from Miss Elizabeth to Mrs. Hurst, whose brows had raised in surprise. "You are a credit to your family, Miss Bingley. Any lady spurned by a gentleman as esteemed as Mr. Darcy would likely find herself tempted towards similar behavior." She patted Miss Bingley's arm. "I do not envy you, my dear."

An expression of pure rage flickered over Miss Bingley's features, but she took a breath and smiled, an overwide smile that revealed the sharp tips of her teeth. "Thank you, Mrs. Bennet. Your generosity of spirit is most gratifying." Miss Bingley's gaze darted to Elizabeth, who was still staring at Miss Bingley as if the lady had sprouted wings and begun to sing. "I hope you can forgive me."

"I—" Elizabeth opened her mouth, and Darcy interjected, "Of course, Miss Bingley. Your candor honors us."

Mrs. Hurst murmured, "Quite so."

Miss Bingley's expression brightened, and she said, "Excellent. I would hate to have ill feelings between us. And as such, I hope you both would humor me by allowing me to host a small gathering in celebration of your upcoming nuptials. Nothing elaborate, only some of the local gentry. Miss Charlotte Lucas is your dear friend, Miss Eliza, is she not?" Without giving Miss Elizabeth a chance to answer, she continued, "And of course, all of you, as well." She smiled, and Darcy thought he saw a flicker of satisfaction in Miss Bingley's blue eyes.

This was an odd turn of events, one Darcy could not bring himself to trust. What was Miss Bingley scheming now? Perhaps, Darcy mused, Miss Bingley had finally accepted the futility of pressing her suit with Darcy and was attempting to smooth things over with him and Miss Elizabeth for the sake of her brother. That seemed a plausible enough scenario, if one accepted Miss Caroline Bingley as a lady who knew when to give up on something she had set her sights on. Nothing in Darcy's experience of the lady proved her inclined to anything of the sort.

So, it had to be something else.

But he could not refuse the lady's invitation without upsetting his friend Bingley, whose loyalty and kindness towards his sister made such rejection impossible. Darcy said, "That would be most gracious of you, Miss Bingley."

"And generous!" Mrs. Bennet chimed in.

"Indeed," Miss Elizabeth said, glancing towards Darcy with a slight frown.

Darcy, knowing himself trapped, ignored the question in her gaze. "We would be delighted to attend your gathering," he said with a forced smile. So long as they took no food or drink directly from Miss Bingley's hand, Darcy doubted a small gathering of this sort could cause further trouble for either him or Miss Elizabeth.

Miss Bingley beamed, and she said, "Wonderful!" She straightened her shoulders and dabbed at her eyes, as if overcome with emotion. "Thank you so much. I will begin planning immediately. Provided the weather holds, an afternoon gathering with tables in the gardens would be the perfect way to celebrate this most joyous occasion."

Miss Lydia giggled and leaned towards Miss Kitty, who nudged her sister's knee, whispering furiously in her ear. Miss Bennet and Jane exchanged a worried glance, and Mr. Bennet, who had remained silent throughout Miss Bingley's speech, merely adjusted his spectacles and took a bite of his tart.

As Mrs. Hurst and Miss Bingley began discussing details, Darcy's unease only grew. He glanced towards Elizabeth, who seemed to share his sentiment. Miss Bingley was up on something. But what?

A knock sounded at the parlor door, interrupting Miss Bingley's discussion of seating arrangements. The footman entered and stammered, "Mr. Bingley, a Lady Catherine de Bourgh of Hunsford, has arrived by carriage. She insists upon speaking to Mr. Darcy at once."

All eyes turned to Darcy, who swallowed.

Clearly, Lady Catherine had learned of the engagement. And Mr. Darcy doubted she was here to offer her congratulations in person. But he had no reason to fear his aunt. The woman might be overbearing and given to pronouncements, but she did not pose a threat to him.

The faint sound of what sounded like Mr. Collins's voice echoed from the hallway, shrill and agitated. Darcy's jaw tightened. Mr. Collins, the bootlicker, must have rushed straight from Longbourn to inform his aunt of Darcy's behavior at the Netherfield ball, and who knew what conclusions his aunt had drawn from the parson's account?

Darcy glanced at his fiancée, who appeared thoughtful. She was a lady of strong opinions and even stronger character, but she deserved neither interrogation nor humiliation from his aunt. Neither did her family, who gaped at Darcy in confusion, clearly expecting some response.

Miss Elizabeth touched his wrist, her fingers cool against his skin, and Darcy's stomach clenched. She said, "I suppose it best we meet with the esteemed lady," and Darcy noticed, to his shock, a glimmer of humor in her gaze. "Mr. Collins has spoken so highly of her."

Darcy choked back an unexpected laugh, his mood lightening at her humor. Miss Elizabeth, it seemed, was unafraid of facing Lady Catherine, and Darcy admired her courage. Unfortunately, it would make more sense for Darcy to meet his aunt alone, at least at first. His aunt was likely to say something unconscionable, and Darcy did not want to subject Miss Elizabeth to her vitriol.

"My aunt asked to speak with me," Darcy said. "I would not force you to bear her ill-temper."

Elizabeth's face flushed. "Mr. Darcy, you make a kind offer, but I suspect I am the cause of her current temper, ill or not. I will stand beside you. We are in this situation together, and we will face it as such."

She straightened, and Darcy, admiring the firm line of her jaw and the fire in her dark eyes, found his good opinion of Miss Elizabeth only strengthening.

Darcy turned to the footman. "Then we shall meet in the day room," he said. "Have my aunt and Mr. Collins wait there until we arrive." The footman bowed and left, and Darcy, steeling himself for whatever insults and accusations awaited them, offered his arm to Miss Elizabeth, who slipped her hand over the crook of his elbow, her fingers curling against his sleeve.

"Come," Darcy said. "Best not to delay the inevitable."

CHAPTER SIXTEEN

Elizabeth, her hand tucked in the crook of Mr. Darcy's arm, wondered if she had made the right decision by insisting on accompanying Mr. Darcy to meet his aunt. Through the half-open doorway, Elizabeth could hear the muffled voices of Lady Catherine and Mr. Collins arguing in the corridor. Lady Catherine, if Elizabeth recalled correctly, was Mr. Darcy's aunt and, according to Mr. Collins's effusive praise, a woman of considerable consequence.

"Well, Lady Catherine de Bourgh. Quite an honor," Mrs. Bennet declared, her gaze darting from Mr. Darcy, who appeared half-furious and half-horrified, to Miss Bingley, who had assumed an air of smug triumph that only intensified Elizabeth's growing dread.

"We will not be long," Elizabeth assured her mother. Jane gave Elizabeth an encouraging smile, while Lydia and Kitty whispered behind their hands. Mary stared, her eyes wide, and Mr. Bennet merely cleared his throat and took a sip of his tea.

As Elizabeth and Mr. Darcy stepped out of the parlor, Mr. Collins's frantic babble grew louder, punctuated by an older woman's voice barking, "Enough, Mr. Collins," her words punctuated by a sharp, thumping sound.

"Mr. Darcy will receive you in the dayroom," the footman said, his voice strained as the older woman, who could only be the estimable Lady Catherine herself, continued in a sour tone, "Nonsense. The butler informed me that my nephew and his chit and her family are in the parlor. I will not idle in a spare room like a common tradesman."

Elizabeth's heart hammered, and her hand tightened around Mr. Darcy's arm as a figure stumbled backwards into the corridor where they stood. The footman, by Elizabeth's recognition, was in full retreat as

Lady Catherine, features regal and cold, advanced, her walking stick striking the floor with each measured step. Mr. Collins jogged at her heels, his face florid, breath puffing as he protested, "Lady Catherine, perhaps it would be best if we—"

"Quiet, Mr. Collins!" Lady Catherine snapped, raising her cane and pointing it at the parson's chest. "I have no patience for your blathering. My nephew will speak to me." Her eyes flashed as she spotted Darcy and Elizabeth standing mere paces ahead of her.

The footman, his hair disheveled and livery rumpled, gave a frantic half-bow. "Mr. Darcy!" he called out with ill-disguised relief.

Mr. Darcy squared his shoulders and said, "Aunt."

"Fitzwilliam," Lady Catherine said, her tone frosty. She planted the tip of her cane against the floor and peered up at him.

Lady Catherine maintained her posture exactly as promised. She stood straight and proud, her features sharp and angular, her hair, though streaked with gray, still glossy and rich. Though her gown was at least five years out of style, it bore the unmistakable air of expense, from the embroidery on the collar and cuffs to the jewels gleaming at her throat and wrists. Her eyes, an icy shade of blue, held a challenge and a hint of malice, and her expression, as she surveyed Elizabeth from head to toe, conveyed a contempt that bordered on disgust.

"Miss Elizabeth Bennet, I presume," Lady Catherine said, her voice crisp and cold.

"It is an honor to meet you at last, Lady Catherine," Elizabeth replied, refusing to break the lady's gaze even as the older woman's lip curled. "My cousin speaks highly of you."

"You could wish the same for yourself." Lady Catherine sniffed, her disdain clear. "But Mr. Collins only speaks highly of those deserving of praise." In a clear dismissal of Elizabeth, she turned her attention to Mr. Darcy and, with a wave of her gloved hand, said, "Fitzwilliam, come. We have much to discuss."

"I assume our conversation concerns my fiancée," Mr. Darcy said, his tone as stony as Elizabeth's nerves had gone wire-tight. "If so, Miss Elizabeth is entitled to hear it."

"Entitled?"

"As my future wife, it is her right," Mr. Darcy said. He raised his chin, and Elizabeth saw his aunt's nostrils flare in indignation.

"I had thought to spare your chit the embarrassment of a tongue-lashing, but I see she lacks the decorum and you the good sense to meet privately." Lady Catherine sneered. "Fine then, let us dispense with pleasantries. Tell me the truth, Fitzwilliam. Have you compromised this young lady, or has she compromised you?"

Elizabeth's temper flared, but before she could respond, Mr. Darcy said, his voice tight with fury, "Miss Elizabeth has done nothing to merit such an accusation."

"Nothing?" Lady Catherine's voice rose to a shriek. "Then explain her behavior at the Netherfield ball. Did she not throw herself upon you like a brazen slattern?"

"She did no such thing." Darcy's face went pale, the muscles in his jaw pulsing. "You will apologize for speaking to my betrothed in such a manner."

"Betrothed!" Lady Catherine scoffed, her gaze flitting to Elizabeth, who refused to look away as the lady continued, "It is a fair question. A poor country miss would do well to compromise herself with one of your status and fortune, nephew."

"Miss Elizabeth is not at fault."

"Mr. Collins, would you say the lady was not at fault?"

"Well— Uhhh—" Mr. Collins's gaze darted between Lady Catherine, Mr. Darcy, and Elizabeth as his color deepened to a worrying shade of purple. "I—" He coughed once, twice, and then descended into a fit of hacking and wheezing.

The sheer ridiculousness of his reaction broke the rising tide of Elizabeth's anger. Lady Catherine could spew what nonsense she chose. She had no more power to change things at this point than Elizabeth or Mr. Darcy. They would wed. And though Elizabeth still thought the love potion, or whatever concoction Mr. Beaumont had sold to Miss Bingley, was to blame for her and Mr. Darcy's behavior at the ball, it could not be responsible for the rest of it. His consideration of her feelings. His strength, steadfastness, and well-hidden sense of humor.

Lady Catherine smirked, a cruel curve of her mouth.

"Surely you do not intend to continue on with this farce, Fitzwilliam. Think of Anne! Think of your own position and how your actions reflect on our family. You cannot marry this woman." She gestured dismissively at Elizabeth.

"And why not?" Elizabeth grinned, the mix of humor and rage sparking the wild sense of rebellion that sometimes made her steal outside in thunderstorms to watch the lightning dance over the sky. "Regarding scandal and compromise, I assure you, Mr. Darcy and I were equally culpable."

"I—! I never—" Lady Catherine stammered.

With a steadying hand on Elizabeth's shoulder, Mr. Darcy said, "Aunt, I believe this discussion is finished."

"Well." Lady Catherine scowled. "Clearly, there is no talking sense into you now. But this is not finished. I am prepared to honor Hertfordshire with my presence until you are prepared to see reason. Or, heaven forbid, you take your marital vows." She turned to the footman, who was still hovering at the end of the hallway. "You—" she jabbed her finger at the man.

"Have my luggage brought inside, and prepare a room for me."

Elizabeth tried not to gape at the lady's audacity, but Mr. Darcy only stiffened beside her, his mouth opening as if to speak.

"Or I suppose I can lodge at Longbourn with Mr. Collins—"

Horror washed over Elizabeth at the thought of hosting Lady Catherine, who had already insulted her and her family to their faces, in their own home. Before Elizabeth could stop herself, she blurted out, "Certainly Netherfield has more suitable accommodations."

Elizabeth locked gazes with Mr. Darcy, imploring him with the tightening of her fingers on his arm to agree. After a long, painful silence, Mr. Darcy nodded, his expression hard. "Of course, Netherfield is more than suited to house you, Aunt. I will speak with Bingley and have him arrange quarters for you." He squeezed Elizabeth's hand, and Elizabeth felt a rush of gratitude towards him. After barely ten minutes with Lady Catherine, she knew hosting the lady for weeks on end was more suffering than Mr. Darcy, or anyone, ought to endure.

"Excellent. I expect no less." Lady Catherine sniffed. "And Fitzwilliam, we will have words later about your behavior, and that of your..." She stared down her nose at Elizabeth. "... Charming companion. But for now, I am fatigued from my journey. Come, Mr. Collins." With no further attempt at courtesy, she made an abrupt turn and strode down the hallway, her walking stick thumping against the floor as Mr. Collins trotted behind her, babbling apologies.

As the echoes of their footsteps faded, Mr. Darcy blew out a heavy breath, and Elizabeth sagged, suddenly exhausted.

Mr. Darcy turned to her and took her hands in his, his gaze earnest. "I am sorry. My aunt is—" He shook his head. "That was far more than you should have had to endure. No matter the nature of our engagement, she had no right to speak to you that way."

"Nor you," Elizabeth returned, feeling a surge of affection for the man who had defended her so fiercely. "We are, as I said, in this together. We will face whatever comes." She leaned in and whispered, "And I dare say you have the worst of it, you and Mr. Bingley, hosting your aunt, and, likely, Mr. Collins for who knows how long. If I had doubted the inherent benevolence of your spirit, Mr. Darcy, you have proven it this day."

Mr. Darcy laughed, a surprised huff that transformed his serious face into a boyish grin. "You are incorrigible, Miss Elizabeth."

"Am I?" Elizabeth returned his grin. Their faces were close enough now that she could feel his breath on her skin. In a moment of daring, she added, "And are you fond of incorrigible ladies?"

"I might be persuaded." Mr. Darcy made to steal another kiss, but at that moment, a portly gentleman Elizabeth recognized as Mr. Hurst, burst into the hallway, declaring, "There is a carriage parked out front, and—!"

Mr. Darcy tensed, releasing Elizabeth's hands. Elizabeth stepped back, her cheeks hot, though she could not tell if it was from shame or desire. She had wanted to kiss Mr. Darcy again, and the realization came with a strange thrill.

Mr. Hurst's eyes widened, and he guffawed, "Oh ho, was I interrupting something?"

"Not at all," Mr. Darcy said stiffly.

Mr. Hurst, still grinning, winked and suggested, "If you cannot manage another ride, perhaps a bracing walk on the grounds is in order?"

"We are well enough, thank you," Mr. Darcy insisted, and Elizabeth nodded her agreement, as though through sheer enthusiasm of bobbing her head she could erase the obvious conclusion Mr. Hurst had already drawn.

Another rush of voices behind them prompted Elizabeth and Mr. Darcy to step back further from each other. The corridor erupted into chaos as Jane and Bingley spilled out of the parlor, followed by Miss Bingley, who glared daggers at Elizabeth and Mr. Darcy, and the rest of Elizabeth's family. Mr. Hurst, still chuckling, called out, "Bingley, are you aware we have guests? Judging from her posture, the fine lady with the walking stick seems set to beat that parson Collins like a mule."

"That is my aunt," Mr. Darcy said, with the joyful expression of one facing a gallows sentence. "She came to... discuss my engagement. And it seems, stay for the wedding. I know it is rather sudden, but Bingley, I would be much obliged if you could have rooms prepared for her."

"Ah." Bingley winced. "Of course."

Mrs. Bennet cried, "How fortunate to be gifted with such esteemed company!" But she lacked her usual enthusiasm, and her fingers fluttered at her throat as if to comfort herself.

"No matter," Mr. Bingley said, clapping Mr. Darcy on the back. "Netherfield is large enough to accommodate another guest. It will be a pleasure."

"It will certainly be an experience," Mr. Hurst said, a sentiment to which Elizabeth could only agree.

CHAPTER SEVENTEEN

The Phillips' dining room, while modest, exuded a certain charm. In the center of the room sat a mahogany table, laden with fresh flowers and polished to a shine. The warm scent of roasting meat filled the air, making Elizabeth's mouth water despite her churning stomach.

Awaiting the meal, Elizabeth stood by the mantelpiece by the window. Charlotte stood beside her, holding a similar pose, but Elizabeth could see that, despite her friend's placid expression, anger and hurt seethed beneath the surface.

Mr. Darcy's proposal, Jane's troubles, and the ongoing mystery of the love potion had preoccupied Elizabeth so much that she had not thought to confide in Charlotte about Mr. Darcy's pursuit of her. Now Elizabeth had hurt her friend's feelings, and she owed it to Charlotte to make amends.

"I did not mean to upset you," Elizabeth blurted.

Charlotte frowned. "I am not upset."

Her friend certainly was upset. Furious even, though she wasn't the sort inclined towards shouting or stamping her feet. Instead, Charlotte revealed her anger through the subtle tightening of her jaw, the quickening of her breath, and the almost imperceptible trembling of her hand resting on the mantel.

Elizabeth tried again to explain. "I should have told you about Mr. Darcy, but it all happened so fast."

Charlotte's fingers tightened on the small plate. "It is not about Mr. Darcy. I am happy for you."

"Charlotte—"

"This is about trust. I thought we were friends." Charlotte's voice wavered. "I have kept nothing from you. Nothing like this."

"I know." And the worst of it was, Elizabeth had kept

nothing from Charlotte either, at least nothing before "the kiss" as Elizabeth had coined the moment in her mind. "It was not a secret. Not like that." She glanced around at the other guests, her mother and Mrs. Phillips by the fireplace, Lydia and Kitty whispering at the table. "I simply—" What could Elizabeth say? Should she mention the love potion? The love potion that might not have been a potion at all. She leaned closer, lowering her voice. "I know you may not believe me, but Mr. Darcy and I were not courting or even remotely interested in each other before Netherfield. At the ball, something happened."

Charlotte's lips thinned, but she allowed Elizabeth to continue. "We do not understand it ourselves. But there is something—" She shivered, remembering Mr. Darcy's lips on hers, his hands in her hair, and the intensity of their passion. "Something strange going on."

Charlotte's gaze flicked towards the ceiling, and Elizabeth realized she might not sound entirely sane. She pressed on, "There is a peddler near the outskirts of the village, a Mr. Beaumont?"

"You have seen him? Has he—" Charlotte sucked in

a sharp breath and Elizabeth realized her friend knew more of the man than she was letting on.

"You bought something from him," Elizabeth guessed.

Charlotte's color heightened, and Elizabeth knew she was correct. "I cannot—. I will not discuss such matters." She moved away, and Elizabeth reached for her, grabbing her arm.

"What was it?"

Charlotte opened her mouth as if to speak, and then closed it, shaking her head. She was paler than Elizabeth had ever seen her, and a fine sheen of sweat dotted her brow.

"Charlotte?" Elizabeth gripped her friend's elbow, concerned. "There is no shame in it, whatever it was." Or hopefully no shame. If Charlotte had also tried to dose some unsuspecting gentleman with a love potion, then Charlotte would have something to be ashamed of, but Elizabeth could not believe her best friend capable of such treachery.

Charlotte glanced over her shoulder, towards where their mothers stood, still chatting, and said, "It was a sachet." She lifted her palm to reveal a small, worn pouch. "Mr. Beaumont claimed it could bring a lady a husband, but—" She swallowed. "I have never believed such things could work."

Elizabeth took the pouch and untied the knot at its top. The smell of dried herbs wafted towards her, and Elizabeth recognized lavender, sage, and other plants whose names she did not know. She sniffed again. There was a slight tang beneath the familiar scents, a bitter, medicinal odor that made her nose wrinkle.

"Why, Charlotte?" Elizabeth asked.

Charlotte's fingers tightened on the pouch as if she were fighting the urge to snatch it back. "It was fool-ishness. I knew it, but I—. I am not like you, Eliza-beth. I am plain and practical. Though my dowry is not insubstantial, I do not attract the attention of eligible gentlemen. I have spent all twenty-seven years of my life living under my parents' roof, and I —. I do not care so much about love. I only want to live my own life. To have a home. A family."

Elizabeth wanted to comfort her friend, but she could not think of anything to say. The truth was,

Charlotte was plain. Elizabeth wanted her friend to marry for affection or even love because her friend deserved to be happy. But Elizabeth could not deny the realities of their world.

Charlotte sighed. "I suppose I cannot blame you for keeping secrets, then. I told you nothing of this." She looked up at Elizabeth with something like hope shining in her eyes. "Did you also purchase a sachet? I know you have always hoped to find affection in marriage, and..." She rubbed her fingers over a cheek gone suddenly pink. "It appeared there was affection between you at the Netherfield ball."

Elizabeth choked on a laugh. Affection was hardly the word for her passionate exchange with Mr. Darcy. And if the potion was not at fault, Elizabeth had no explanation for their behavior despite the growing feelings she had for him. Feelings that surpassed mere affection if she were being honest with herself.

Elizabeth handed the pouch back to Charlotte and said, "No, I bought nothing from Mr. Beaumont."

"Oh." Charlotte's shoulders slumped as she slid the sachet back into the folds of her gown. "It is a good thing then that I did not take one of his potions, I suppose. Yet he seemed an honest sort for one of his profession. The potions cost a good deal more coin than a sachet, but he insisted I need not purchase one. He said it would be wholly unsuitable."

"I have heard his potions are just as unreliable," Elizabeth said. She glanced around, and seeing no one standing close enough to overhear, added in a whisper, "But I think Miss Bingley purchased one and gave it to Mr. Darcy."

Charlotte laughed, her eyes glittering with a more malicious edge than Elizabeth usually saw in her friend. "If she did, I hope she demanded her payment returned."

Elizabeth chuckled, feeling some of the tension between them ease. "Yes, indeed. Mr. Darcy and I went to call on Mr. Beaumont, but his wagon was missing. A passing beggar" —or poor tenant, Elizabeth could not be sure—"was certain Mr. Beaumont is a fraud, and Mr. Jones has much the same opinion. But..." Elizabeth shrugged. "It was an odd thing. Mr. Darcy claims he was quite overcome."

"Perhaps he had secretly fallen in love with you,"

Charlotte said, a mischievous smirk twitching at the corners of her mouth. "And Miss Bingley's potion only revealed his true feelings."

"That is almost as ridiculous as the idea that a potion could make someone fall in love at all," Elizabeth retorted. "Besides, if that was the case, I must also have been secretly in love with the gentleman, and that I cannot believe."

"Hmm." Charlotte tilted her head as if considering. "It seems unlikely."

"Yes." Elizabeth agreed, but a part of her couldn't escape the niggling sensation that maybe her friend was right.

Charlotte glanced over Elizabeth's shoulder, and she asked, "Is that Mr. Collins? I thought he had gone back to Hunsford?"

Elizabeth sighed. "He returned to Hertfordshire with his patroness, Mr. Darcy's aunt, who is about as disagreeable a lady as I have ever encountered." She shook her head. "Lady Catherine is at Netherfield and Mr. Collins at Longbourn until the wedding." Or until Mr. Collins's ham-fisted attempts to convince Elizabeth to break the engagement bore fruit, which Elizabeth determined would happen sometimes after flaming toads rained from the sky.

Mr. Collins's badgering had forced Elizabeth to wake and leave Longbourn nearly at dawn with a basket of food to escape the parson's prying questions. And worse, his lectures. It had been all she could manage not to lose her temper in the carriage on the way to her aunt and uncle Phillips.

Charlotte grimaced, and Elizabeth agreed with her silent sentiment. "He is coming this way."

"Please, if you still have any feelings of friendship towards me," Elizabeth begged. "Distract him. Ask him about Hunsford or his patroness or —"

"You have no other great secrets, I trust? The prince regent is not your secret father?"

"No!" Elizabeth laughed.

Charlotte straightened her shoulders. "Then, once more unto the breach as they say." She walked towards Mr. Collins and called out his name. The parson froze, as startled as a deer at the sound of buckshot.

Elizabeth breathed a sigh of relief as she skirted

behind Charlotte and towards the fireplace or anywhere Mr. Collins was not. She had made it halfway towards the parlor when she was stopped by a gentleman's voice. "Miss Elizabeth?"

Elizabeth whirled to face Mr. Wickham. She had not spoken to him since the last dinner at her aunt and uncle's, and he smiled. It was a handsome smile on a handsome face, but Elizabeth felt little more than curiosity at why he had deliberately sought her out.

"Mr. Wickham," she returned, trying to keep her tone light. At least he would not bore her to death with sermons on propriety or beg her to reconsider her engagement to Mr. Darcy for the twentieth time. And he had grown up with Mr. Darcy. Though when they had last spoken, Mr. Wickham had not given a favorable account of the man.

"I must say, Miss Elizabeth, you look most fetching tonight," Mr. Wickham said.

Kiss aside, he had done nothing to earn her distrust, and Mr. Wickham, while charming, had offered no evidence to support his earlier accusations. Vague accusations. Unfounded accusations, Elizabeth suspected. But as she faced the gentleman, her curiosity about those accusations and Mr. Darcy's life before coming to Netherfield grew.

It could not hurt to speak with the gentleman. To learn about her future husband from someone who had known him during a different time in his life.

Elizabeth smiled and said, "Thank you, Mr. Wickham. Shall we have a seat?" She gestured at a pair of chairs by the window.

"Of course. I hoped we would find an opportunity to speak." He gestured for Elizabeth to lead the way, and as she did, questions tumbled through Elizabeth's mind.

What if there was a grain of truth in Mr. Wickham's accusations against Mr. Darcy? What would that mean for Elizabeth's future marriage and happiness?

CHAPTER EIGHTEEN

When Darcy arrived in the stables an hour after dawn, Lady Catherine was already there, pacing back and forth between the stalls, her cane tapping the packed earth of the aisle. She turned sharply as Darcy approached, her lips pursed, and her eyes narrowed in a glare. "Fitzwilliam Darcy."

"Aunt Catherine." Mr. Darcy bowed. It was hours earlier than his aunt would normally rise, which meant she had awakened and come here deliberately. "If you would excuse me. My horse is ready to be saddled."

"Then we shall ride together," Lady Catherine declared.

Darcy suppressed a shudder. His aunt was a terrible rider, and her presence on horseback would only make his own riding that much harder. Darcy would have to match her pace and make sure she did not veer into a ditch or a pond. Worse, she despised it, not that she would admit as much. She would insist upon riding, regardless of her skills or the risk, to prove a point.

"It is early, and you mentioned your leg was causing you some trouble last night at dinner."

Lady Catherine drew herself up to her full height and said, "If the only way I can command my nephew's attention is on horseback, then I will suffer through it." She motioned to the groom, who had been hovering nearby, to fetch her mount.

Darcy sighed. As he could not avoid this conversation, it would be better to have it on the ground than midair. "We will take a stroll in the garden," Darcy said. "It will be more comfortable for us both." And safer.

"I am perfectly capable of riding." Lady Catherine protested, again gesturing for the groom.

Darcy considered agreeing to it. Lady Catherine would be far less capable of causing him trouble with a broken leg, but such a thought was ungentlemanly. And Darcy was a gentleman. Not to mention, he would never hear the end of it if his aunt suffered some injury while attempting to instill in him the wisdom of ending his engagement to Miss Elizabeth.

"Of course you are capable," Darcy said. "But conversation will be easier afoot, and the dahlias are especially lovely this time of year. Netherfield boasts a beautiful display."

Lady Catherine eyed Darcy, clearly weighing her options. Finally, with a dismissive sniff, she said, "Very well."

Darcy ordered the groom to return the horses to their stall, and he and his aunt left the stables and walked in silence around the perimeter of the extensive Netherfield grounds.

The smell of autumn leaves filled Darcy's nostrils, and he savored the crisp tang of it, mixed with the sweetness of blooming chrysanthemums and the smoky musk of damp earth. Chirping birdsong and the rustling of branches overhead punctuated the silence, but Darcy was on edge, waiting for his aunt's inevitable outburst.

Lady Catherine walked with purpose, her cane tapping the ground with each step, her spine as stiff as iron. Finally, she spoke, her tone haughty, "Your behavior, Fitzwilliam, has not gone unnoticed."

"Certainly not." Darcy let out a bitter laugh. "But Miss Elizabeth and I are engaged to wed, so there is no concern."

"Engaged perhaps, but not yet married." Lady Catherine paused at the edge of a flowerbed. The dahlias Darcy had referenced swayed gently in the breeze, their blooms a riot of color, reds, yellows, and oranges that reminded Darcy of a bonfire. "And I wonder what your father would say if he were alive. Would he approve of this arrangement, or would he be ashamed of how you have thrown yourself away on a penniless, untitled nobody?"

Darcy clenched his fists at his sides and reminded himself to breathe. "My engagement to Miss Elizabeth has no bearing on my inheritance. And my father would be proud of the honorable choice I have made."

Lady Catherine sniffed. It was more of a snort, really, but his aunt never admitted to such base gestures and resented those who acknowledged them. "I do not doubt your honor, Fitzwilliam, so you can shake those storm clouds from your expression. What I doubt is your judgment."

"My judgment is fine." Darcy retorted, "Miss Elizabeth is an intelligent, vivacious woman, who, while not born to the same wealth as I, will be a credit to our family."

"Our family." Lady Catherine struck her cane against the line of stones edging the path. "You had no intention of marrying Miss Elizabeth Bennet until the moment she suborned you into such a disgraceful display. I never thought you, of all my relations, would succumb to a fortune hunter."

"Miss Elizabeth is not a fortune hunter," Darcy snapped, his temper threatening to boil over. "She is a clever, spirited woman, and while she is not from a titled family, she is well-educated and well-mannered, far more so than you have given her credit for."

"Insolence." Lady Catherine hissed. She reached out

and jabbed her cane into the ground at Darcy's feet, forcing him a step back. "Do you believe the rumors that Miss Elizabeth threw herself at you at the ball, a blatant attempt to trap you into marriage?"

Darcy blinked, shocked at the accusation. Miss Elizabeth had kissed him as fervently as he had kissed her, but that did not mean—.

But what if it meant... something?

A compromise to a lady of far less means than himself, one who lacked any fortune whatsoever, could certainly be for monetary gain. Darcy could not believe Miss Elizabeth had schemed to ensnare him, but...

"Finally, you are thinking with the head above your shoulders," Lady Catherine said, her gaze triumphant. "You cannot possibly marry this woman now. She will drain your accounts dry and spend your fortune on frivolities, and you will be left a pauper, alone and with no one to blame but yourself."

But Elizabeth had been just as eager as he to find the peddler and get to the truth of Miss Bingley's actions. She did not act as one who wanted to trap a wealthy, respectable gentleman into marriage. Darcy did not want to believe the worst of her. He was far too enamored, fallen nearly as far as Bingley into the throes of new love.

Lady Catherine's voice softened, and her expression was almost tender as she said, "You had no intentions of marrying this girl until that ill-advised kiss, did you?"

"We were engaged to wed," Darcy repeated, stubbornly.

"If you had made plans to marry her, you would have spoken with my brother, the Earl," his aunt never called her brother by name, instead referring to him as 'my brother, the Earl,' "to request a Special License from the Bishop of Canterbury. And lacking that, you would at least have gotten a Common License and spared yourself the three weeks reading of the banns. You did neither of those things. Instead, you have opted for a commoner's ceremony. It is clear that you are not fully committed to this match, and you owe it to yourself, and to Miss Elizabeth, to end it now, before you make a grave mistake. Lady Catherine adjusted her grip on her cane and added, "The lady will surely be persuaded to put aside the engagement with sufficient financial incentive. Especially as I have heard you were not her only suitor."

The words hit Darcy like a blow to the stomach. Miss Elizabeth had another suitor? Perhaps his aunt meant Mr. Collins? The parson, Miss Elizabeth's cousin for heaven's sake, hardly counted. But the slight twitch at the corner of his aunt's mouth and the gleam in her eyes made Darcy think she was hinting at another gentleman. A secret gentleman. One that Elizabeth had not shared with Darcy, even after their passionate embrace and time spent together since.

It could not be true.

Knowing no good would come from questioning but feeling compelled to do so anyway, Darcy asked, "What gentleman?"

Lady Catherine smiled, her teeth bared, predatory. "A militia officer, newly stationed here. I do not have a name, but from what I understand, he is quite handsome. Fair-haired and pleasant natured."

A vague description that could be almost anyone in the Hertfordshire militia. Even George Wickham.

The thought of that scoundrel laying a hand on Miss Elizabeth flared Darcy's temper to new heights. Darcy already despised Wickham for his attempted seduction of Georgiana, not to mention the fortune he had squandered in gambling halls. But if Wickham had designs on Miss Elizabeth...

No. It made no sense. George Wickham's interest in marriage began and ended with the size of a lady's fortune. And Miss Elizabeth was not the sort to engage in a dalliance for the sake of pleasure. She was far too principled, too smart, and too determined to secure a match based on genuine affection and mutual respect. She had made that abundantly clear.

"As delightful as this conversation has been," Darcy said, his voice thick with sarcasm. "I cannot ignore the demands of my responsibilities.

"From what I have heard, the gentleman is a friend of Miss Elizabeth's aunt and uncle. They have been seen together, more than once, speaking intimately."

Darcy's pulse quickened, and he hated himself for feeling jealous. Miss Elizabeth had no obligation to inform him of every gentleman who paid her a compliment or tried to engage her in conversation. Still, the thought of her laughing with another man, sharing secrets, or exchanging glances, twisted Darcy's gut, making him feel ill.

And if it was George Wickham?

"Are you certain you do not know the gentleman's name? If there is gossip, such information should be readily available." Darcy did not trust his aunt to be entirely truthful, but she enjoyed a good scandal and would revel in bringing down Miss Elizabeth's reputation, even if it was false.

Lady Catherine pursed her lips, and her brows lowered in obvious irritation. "It would be easier if I did. But the lady who spoke to me, a close friend from my understanding, said she was sworn to secrecy. I know only that it is a gentleman in the Hertfordshire militia."

"What friend?" Miss Elizabeth was close with her sister Jane and Charlotte Lucas. But why would either of them have shared this information with his aunt?

Lady Catherine shook her head. "I will not break a confidence." She tapped her cane to emphasize her point. "But as difficult as it may be for you to accept, it is possible your Miss Elizabeth is not as innocent and virtuous as you believe. If she has designs on your fortune, you have made it all too easy for her."

"I do not believe she has such designs," Darcy said stiffly, but the seed of doubt had been planted. And as much as he wanted to root it out, he could not entirely dismiss his aunt's words.

Lady Catherine inclined her head. "In the end, the decision is yours, Fitzwilliam. And you must decide if Miss Elizabeth is truly worthy of your devotion. Think carefully before you commit to a marriage that will haunt you for the rest of your life. Now," she waved a hand back in the direction they had come. "You wished to ride, and I should like to return to Netherfield and freshen up before breakfast."

Darcy, trained towards politeness even as his entire body burned with a mix of confusion and fury, nodded and offered his arm to his aunt.

"Neither you nor I are in a state for pleasantries," Lady Catherine declared. "Be about your ride and think about what we discussed." With that, she adjusted her grip on her walking stick and set off back towards the manor house, leaving Darcy to stare after her, wondering how he had become entangled in this mess. And if Miss Elizabeth had, indeed, betrayed his trust.

And the worst of it was the niggling possibility that whispered in his mind. One he could not conscience himself to believe, even as he desperately worked to root it from his mind. What if Miss Elizabeth had not only betrayed his trust, but betrayed it with George Wickham?

CHAPTER NINETEEN

Mr. Wickham leaned back on the sofa, one arm draped casually across the cushions, his fingertips nearly brushing Elizabeth's shoulder in a manner she found increasingly bold. His expression was one of solemnity, though, as he held her gaze, blue eyes shining with intent. "If Mr. Darcy is, as it seems, a changed man, I can only credit it to your influence, Miss Elizabeth."

Elizabeth resisted the urge to roll her eyes at the flattery. Mr. Wickham could not know how little influence Elizabeth had over Mr. Darcy. Despite their engagement, Elizabeth held no real sway over Mr. Darcy's thoughts or beliefs, especially regarding Mr. Wickham, whose name had not surfaced during any of their conversations. And even if Miss Bingley's love potion had compelled her and Mr. Darcy's first kiss, she doubted the effects of a charlatan's brew would encompass every aspect of Mr. Darcy's behavior.

"I cannot take credit for whatever changes Mr. Darcy may have undergone," Elizabeth said, shifting away from Mr. Wickham and his overly familiar attitude. "Though I must admit, I have found him to be a much more considerate and open-minded individual than I expected."

"That is high praise, indeed," Mr. Wickham said. "I never believed Mr. Darcy could change, not in the ways that count, but it is possible you have worked a miracle."

"How exactly did Mr. Darcy wrong you?" Elizabeth asked, her frustration at Mr. Wickham's half-truths and implications finally forcing her to directness.

Mr. Wickham's smile faltered, and he ran a finger along the buttoned seam of the sofa as though to distract himself. "It is an old wound, and one I cannot speak of lightly." He looked up, his gaze meeting hers, and Elizabeth was surprised by the sadness she saw reflected there. "It pains me to speak of it, but I will, for I believe you are deserving of the truth."

"Go on," Elizabeth prompted, not trusting Mr. Wickham's sudden sincerity or the idea that he was about to share the secrets he had so far kept to himself.

"You see, Mr. Darcy and I grew up together at Pemberley, his family's estate. He was like a brother to me, and I, like a brother to him, at least until—" Mr. Wickham sighed, his shoulders slumping as if reliving a painful memory. "It was a long time ago. Mr. Darcy cut ties with me and denied me the inheritance that should have been mine. It was a betrayal, and one I will never forget."

Despite Elizabeth's suspicions, this revelation intrigued her. Mr. Darcy had never mentioned cutting ties with Mr. Wickham. He had not spoken of their childhood friendship at all. Elizabeth tried to imagine Mr. Wickham and Mr. Darcy as children, playing in the grass and chasing rabbits. Or perhaps having adventures. It was a sweet thought, but not one she could reconcile with the gentleman sitting beside her now, his handsome features hardened by bitterness.

"Mr. Darcy has not mentioned this to me," Elizabeth said, trying to keep her tone neutral.

"It is not something he would advertise, not with his pride and his desire to appear always right and infallible."

Before her and Mr. Darcy's kiss, their conversations, and their visit to Mr. Beaumont, Elizabeth might have swallowed Mr. Wickham's words whole. But now, after getting to know Mr. Darcy, after seeing a glimpse of the man beneath his aloof exterior, she was not so certain.

Still, there would be no harm in learning more about his and Mr. Darcy's relationship.

Mr. Wickham said, "I suspect he believes you would not understand, that you would judge him harshly for his choices." He glanced over Elizabeth's shoulder, where Mr. Collins was pontificating to Charlotte with increasing enthusiasm on the topic of marriage and matrimony. "He likely fears your opinion of him."

"And what of your opinion of him?" Elizabeth asked. "Do you believe him a cruel and callous gentleman?"

"No, not entirely." Mr. Wickham sighed again, and Elizabeth could almost believe the regret she saw in his eyes. "Mr. Darcy and I had a falling out, and he ignored his father's wishes and denied me what was rightfully mine." He straightened, his jaw tightening. "I cannot claim to have been entirely without fault. But Mr. Darcy is wealthy, powerful, and he has used those advantages to crush those who dared stand in his way. I had always believed he would do it again if the situation suited him. You have not seen this side of him, have you?"

Elizabeth thought back over all her interactions with Mr. Darcy, both recently and before their engagement. He was, by most people's standards, aloof, but not unkind. He had been respectful to her and her family, even when they had been less so to him. And while he sometimes rushed to conclusions, he also apologized for his mistakes and admitted his failings. She saw nothing of the hard gentleman Mr. Wickham described in the person she had agreed to marry.

"No," Elizabeth said. "I have not seen it."

"Good," Mr. Wickham said, a hint of a smile

returning to his expression. "Then it seems you may have tamed the beast after all."

Elizabeth blinked, not liking Mr. Wickham's implication that she had somehow subdued Mr. Darcy's darker nature. As though the gentleman had a darker nature.

But Mr. Wickham continued without seeming to notice Elizabeth's discomfort. "Given a chance, I would like to make amends. Not that he would receive me, of course." He rubbed a palm over his cheek, and Elizabeth wondered at the slight trembling she saw in his fingers.

"I cannot say." And Elizabeth had no intention of ruining Mr. Darcy's good opinion of her by attempting to broker a meeting between him and someone he despised.

Mr. Wickham sighed. "I would not ask you to involve yourself in such matters. But perhaps, if I were to find myself in Mr. Darcy's presence, you could encourage him to hear me out. I have much to apologize for and much to regret. And if I could make even a small measure of reparation—" He shook his head. "It is too much to ask, I know."

It was too much to ask, but she doubted Mr. Wickham and Mr. Darcy would ever find themselves in each other's company, so Elizabeth merely nodded. "I cannot promise anything, but should the opportunity arise, I will do what I can."

"Thank you, Miss Elizabeth," Mr. Wickham said. He reached over and took Elizabeth's hand, holding it a beat longer than was proper. "I appreciate your kindness."

Elizabeth pulled her hand away, unnerved by Mr. Wickham's touch and the intensity of his gaze. She was suddenly aware that Mr. Collins had moved closer, Charlotte at his side, and that they were both watching her and Mr. Wickham with expressions of confusion and suspicion.

Mr. Phillips rose, and, tapping a fork to the edge of his glass, invited them to take seats at the dining table for their meal. Elizabeth stood, and, with a nod, made her way towards the table, grateful to escape Mr. Wickham's unsettling company. Charlotte took the chair beside her. As they sat down, she leaned in and asked, "What was that about?"

Elizabeth shrugged, unsure how to explain her

conversation with Mr. Wickham when she was still sorting out her own feelings on the matter.

She had agreed to help Mr. Wickham make his case to Mr. Darcy, but she could not say that she trusted Mr. Wickham or his version of events. More than anything, she hoped never to have to keep her promise. But Elizabeth could not escape the lingering worry that her promise, made mostly in politeness, would come around to bite her at the worst possible moment.

CHAPTER TWENTY

Fortunately, or unfortunately, Darcy had yet to decide, the weather held fair and unseasonably warm for Miss Bingley's outdoor gathering to celebrate his and Miss Elizabeth's engagement. Darcy had the window cracked, and a cool breeze blew through the curtains, bringing with it the sharp sounds of his aunt's raised voice ordering the servants about and Miss Bingley's equally sharp tones directing the placement of refreshments.

Darcy closed his eyes, wishing he could vanish into the ether and avoid the uncomfortable gathering ahead. But Miss Bingley had created the affair in his and Miss Elizabeth's honor, and Darcy could not repudiate her efforts to mend fences. He would attend and endure the awkward conversations and barely concealed criticisms with his best attempt at civility.

Darcy's valet had just finished helping Darcy dress when Bingley burst through the door, his face flushed. "Darcy, thank goodness you're here. I need your advice."

"Advice?" From the longing looks and scraps of ill-rhyming poetry Darcy had seen scattered around Bingley's study, he had a good idea of exactly what advice his friend sought, and he feared Bingley's infatuation with Miss Bennet was just that, infatuation.

Bingley paced the room, running a hand through his wavy brown hair. "Yes, advice." He took a deep breath, and throwing his hand wide, said, "I want to ask Jane. Today."

Darcy quirked an eyebrow. "Ask her about the weather? Or the state of her health? Or to pass the butter dish at dinner?"

Bingley rolled his eyes. "I want to propose."

Of course he did. Bingley was nothing if not honorable. And seeing Darcy happily engaged to Miss Elizabeth must have prodded him to act. But Bingley wore infatuation the way other gentlemen sported a perfectly starched cravat, and Darcy worried his friend would regret hasty choices. "Have you given enough consideration to the matter?"

"Yes." Bingley stopped his pacing and faced Darcy, his expression earnest. "I have considered everything, and Jane is perfect. She is kind and intelligent and—" He shook his head. "More importantly, I am not willing to lose her to another."

Darcy sighed. Miss Jane Bennet was a sensible woman, and if she returned Bingley's feelings, his proposal would likely be well received. But what if his friend's infatuation drove him into a hasty and ill-thought-out engagement? And Darcy had no room to express such a worry, given his own behavior where Miss Elizabeth was concerned. The memory of their kiss flashed through Darcy's mind, and he shuddered, remembering the heat of Miss Elizabeth's lips against his, the press of her body, and the fire that had ignited between them.

Had she had another suitor even then? His aunt claimed it was a rumor, but if it was true, Elizabeth had kept it from him. Darcy did not want to believe it, but his aunt's accusations had opened a crack in his armor, and he could not seem to force it shut. The doubt gnawed at him like a splinter buried under his skin.

Darcy shook his head. He needed to focus on Bingley's problem, not his own. "Are you sure, Bingley? Have you considered the implications of asking for her hand, especially after Miss Elizabeth and I—"

"I have considered all of that." Bingley sank into the chair near the window with a heavy sigh, the brocade upholstery creaking under his weight. His shoulders were tense, his fingers drumming on the armrest. "I care for her, Darcy, more than I ever thought possible. And I will risk public censure or mockery if it means I can spend my life with her. As you risked for Miss Elizabeth."

Darcy winced at the truth in his friend's words. "It is not the same," he protested weakly, though he had no way to explain the difference without accusing Bingley's sister of doctoring his drink with an illicit potion. "Miss Elizabeth and I..." He let out an exhausted sigh, pressing his fingertips to his temple. "We suit each other well. At least, I believe we do."

The words rang hollow, even to his own ears. If Miss Elizabeth's heart belonged to another...?

Bingley rose to his feet, face flushed with anger. "You have no place to question my actions or my affections after the display you and Miss Elizabeth made at the ball."

Stung, Darcy opened his mouth to respond, but Bingley barreled on. "I thought you would wish me well, Darcy. And instead, you—" He broke off with a frustrated gesture before stalking to the door. "Forget it. You do not have to approve. I will ask her, regardless."

Darcy stepped forward, "Bingley—"

Bingley hesitated, and Darcy swallowed his reservations and said, "I will always wish you well. All I want is your happiness. And if you believe Miss Bennet will bring you happiness, then I support you."

The tension in Bingley's shoulders eased. "Thank you, Darcy. That means a great deal." He grinned and clapped Darcy on the arm. "Especially as I need your help."

Darcy returned his smile, ignoring the knot of unease in his stomach. "How?"

Bingley explained his plan as they walked together down the corridor. "All I need is for you to hold her parents' attention. Especially her father's, until I can pull Jane aside."

While Darcy was not excited about spending more time with Miss Elizabeth's father, considering the conversation they had had in the library, he owed Bingley. And if Darcy directed his questioning well enough, he might learn more about Miss Elizabeth's other suitors, and discover if his aunt was right and his fiancée was playing him for a fool.

"I will do what I can," Darcy said.

"Thank you," Bingley said as they headed outside.

The air was crisp, and Darcy took a deep breath, savoring the fragrant air with the scent of apples overlaying the muskier, sharper smells of damp earth and fallen leaves. He and Bingley walked in silence, lost in their respective concerns. A cluster of dahlias, bright red and orange, caught Darcy's eye, and he imagined Miss Elizabeth gathering them in her slender hands, her eyes sparkling with laughter as she presented them to him.

But would she? Or would she be planning her next rendezvous with some mysterious gentleman while Darcy played the oblivious suitor?

Darcy clenched his jaw, his muscles jumping in his cheek, as they reached the garden area where the tables were arranged. Mr. Hurst stood, his hand cupped over his eyes as he stared out at the fields beyond the fence, as if hoping for an excuse to flee the gathering before it had even begun. Mr. Darcy suppressed a sympathetic chuckle. Darcy could not blame him for wanting an escape. Mrs. Hurst, in contrast, engaged in a lively interchange with Lady Lucas, who had arrived early with her two daughters. Her eldest, Charlotte Lucas, wore a placid smile as she stood beside Mr. Collins, her gaze a bit unfocused as he droned on about something Darcy could not quite make out from this distance.

As Darcy and Bingley approached, Darcy spotted Lady Catherine and Miss Bingley conversing with surprising familiarity, and he stifled a groan. While Lady Catherine and Miss Bingley were both self-centered and ambitious, Lady Catherine had a particular loathing for social climbers. Miss Bingley, with her lust for wealth and status, should be anathema to Lady Catherine's sensibilities. And yet they sat together, heads bowed in discussion, Lady Catherine's expression cold but not outright hostile, while Miss Bingley's expression was one of excitement and eagerness.

Miss Bingley waved, calling out his and her brother's name, "Charles! Mr. Darcy!" She set aside an inkwell and quill, placing a stone over a small stack of papers, and rose to her feet, smoothing her skirts, as Lady Catherine turned her piercing gaze towards Darcy, her lips pressed into a thin line.

Darcy and Bingley approached, and Miss Bingley gestured to the empty chairs. "Please join us. It would be nice to chat before the bulk of our guests arrive."

Lady Catherine inclined her head regally, her eyes gleaming. A parasol rested beside her on the ground, and Darcy assumed she had been using it to shade her delicate skin from the unseasonable autumn sun.

Darcy took a seat, Bingley sinking into the chair

beside him with a polite greeting, while Lady Catherine eyed Darcy, her expression inscrutable.

Miss Bingley wore a gown of pale pink silk, and while it was a beautiful color on her, it reminded Darcy of a piece of candy or a sweet confection that was more show than substance. She chattered brightly, discussing her letter writing, the arrangements, the weather, and a new hat she had purchased in London, which she had not yet had the opportunity to wear.

Darcy tuned out the conversation, his attention focused on the incoming carriages, watching for the distinctive form of the Bennet carriage. He longed to speak with Miss Elizabeth, to clear the air between them and confirm that there was nothing between her and another gentleman. And all this aside, he longed to see her smile and tease him, to laugh with her, and hold her hand.

Lady Catherine cleared her throat, and Darcy realized she had been speaking to him. "Mr. Darcy, I was inquiring as to your plans for the wedding breakfast. I assume you will have it at Netherfield?"

"Indeed, he will," Miss Bingley said with an overabundance of cheer. "Charles and I would be delighted to host, and—"

"I see." Lady Catherine shot Miss Bingley a glare before she schooled her features back to an approximation of calm.

What were the two of them plotting?

Before Darcy could put more thought into the question, he spotted the faded blue paint of the Bennet carriage lumbering down the lane. Miss Bingley stood, exclaiming something that Darcy barely acknowledged. Then she stumbled, practically falling into his lap. Instinctively, Darcy grabbed her to steady her as something wet slapped against the side of his neck. It tickled, dripping like a warm, tingling honey to soak into his cravat. Darcy swiped at it and held his hand out to see his fingers stained black.

"Oh!" Miss Bingley's eyes went as wide as saucers, and she scrambled up with a cry of seeming distress that grated against Darcy's nerves. "How clumsy of me! I had been writing out the final place settings and..." She blinked her blue eyes rapidly as though she would burst into tears, but Darcy saw no trace of them. "It is such a disaster." She dabbed at his collar with her lace kerchief, her expression horrified. "You will have to change."

Darcy stood, his irritation rising, as Miss Bingley fussed and fretted, and Lady Catherine watched with a satisfied gleam in her eye. No matter her protestations, Darcy felt Miss Bingley had intended to spill ink on him. Why, Darcy could not guess, but he had little patience for her manipulations, especially with Miss Elizabeth about to arrive.

Miss Bingley hovered, her tone apologetic, but Darcy was already walking away, his steps quick and determined, his gut twisting with uncertainty and growing rage. The faster he changed, the faster he could return to meet his fiancée.

Whatever Miss Bingley had intended by this ruse, Darcy refused to let it distract him from his true purpose. He would see Miss Elizabeth and get to the truth, even if it meant confronting her directly and revealing his fears, his doubts, and his hopes.

Even if it meant losing her forever.

CHAPTER TWENTY-ONE

"A party in honor of our Lizzy's engagement! When Lady Lucas received the invitation, she must have been fit to birth kittens!" Mrs. Bennet repeated for what felt like the hundredth time since the official invitation had arrived. And perhaps the twentieth since they had entered this carriage. "If I could have been a fly on that wall, to see Lady Lucas's reaction, I would have enjoyed it immensely.

Mrs. Bennet sighed, leaning back against the plush cushion. "But I could not contrive to visit at the moment the invitation arrived, and Lady Lucas claimed a megrim the very next day. Not that she is prone to megrims, though I suppose we could term this a megrim of misery, poor dear..." Mrs. Bennet's words of sympathy held more than a thread of glee. "It is abundantly clear her daughters Charlotte and Maria are inferior to our Jane and Elizabeth. No matter how it makes her head ache, she cannot claim offense by that comparison. She cannot!"

Elizabeth rolled her eyes and exchanged a knowing glance with Jane, who sat across from her. Jane gave her a reassuring smile, but Elizabeth could see the tension in her older sister's shoulders and the stiffness of her spine. Jane did not like conflict, and they would face a world of it with Mrs. Bennet's boundless enthusiasm and Lady Lucas's indignation. Not to mention Jane's courtship with Mr. Bingley, which had been wholly overshadowed by Elizabeth and Mr. Darcy's scandal.

Last night, Jane had expressed the fear that though Mr. Bingley remained cordial and even solicitous, he showed no signs of deeper interest. Perhaps his affections had cooled? She had not seen him in several days, and while Caroline Bingley's estate business dominated her brother's time, Jane worried Mr. Bingley had decided against a union, feeling too ashamed of the gossip swirling around Elizabeth and Mr. Darcy.

Jane had seemed ready to give up on the gentleman entirely, but Elizabeth had refused to let her sister throw away her own happiness. "I am certain our parents will remain focused on Mr. Darcy and me, and that will give you and Mr. Bingley the chance for a private word without risking censure," Elizabeth had said. And with careful prodding, she had convinced Jane to attend today's gathering and speak to Mr. Bingley in private.

They passed a poplar grove, the branches nearly bare, the tree skeletons reaching towards the sky, and Elizabeth gazed out the window, lost in thought. She had not seen Mr. Darcy since her aunt and uncle's dinner party and her troubling conversation with Mr. Wickham, and she wanted to speak with Mr. Darcy to let him know of Mr. Wickham's claims and the possibility of the gentleman seeking amends.

Mr. Bennet, seated at Elizabeth's opposite side, well away from his own wife, leaned toward Elizabeth and in a low tone, said, "It seems your young gentleman is making an effort."

Elizabeth nodded. If someone had asked her a week ago if she would think of Mr. Darcy with fondness or anticipate seeing him with something like pleasure, she would have laughed incredulously. But here they were. And if she were honest, she was looking forward to speaking with Mr. Darcy. She wanted to tease him about his aunt's dramatics and listen to his wry observations and laugh with him, as they had done before.

Before.

Her heart ached, and she pushed away thoughts of Mr. Wickham's claims and her own worries. Mr. Darcy was a good man, and while she might never have seen past his pride without Miss Bingley's potion or whatever movement of the stars or spheres that had compelled their kiss, she did not regret it.

As they approached Netherfield, Elizabeth sucked in a steadying breath. She would soon see Mr. Darcy again, and all would be well. It must be.

Elizabeth peered through the window, searching for Mr. Darcy. But he was nowhere in sight. She frowned, disappointment churning in her stomach. Was this not a planned gathering to celebrate their engagement? What reason would Mr. Darcy have to avoid it? She squared her shoulders, trying to ignore the tightness in her chest and the knot in her throat. He was here. He had to be. She had no cause for concern.

But her worries only grew as the carriage slowed and her family alighted. Mr. Bingley was there, his smile a touch strained as he held his hand out to Jane to help down. Miss Bingley stood at her brother's side, her expression a mask of welcome, though Elizabeth saw the calculation in her eyes as their gazes met.

A footman waited to assist Elizabeth, and she forced a smile as he helped her from the carriage. She joined her sisters on the drive, taking in the immaculate lawn, the colorful garden beds, and the glittering pond in the distance. Tables had been arranged on the green, their white linen tablecloths snapping in the breeze. Servants bustled about, carrying platters of food and drink and adjusting the chairs. Mr. Darcy's estimable aunt, Lady Catherine, walked from the tables towards them, her expression severe. She wore a dark lavender gown, the fabric shimmering in the sunlight, a matching parasol gripped firmly in one hand, her cane in the other. She looked every inch a dowager noblewoman, imperious and intimidating.

Elizabeth braced herself for whatever criticism or insult Lady Catherine was about to unleash. But halfway to the group, a maid intercepted her. The two exchanged words, and Lady Catherine turned abruptly towards the main house, marching back inside with a hurriedness that suggested something urgent awaited her attention.

"Mrs. and Mrs. Bennet," Miss Bingley said, sweeping the skirts of her pink gown aside in an elegant curtsy. "It is an honor to host you both. And of course, Miss Elizabeth and your wealth of daughters."

Miss Bingley's tone was cordial and her words just shy of an insult, but Mrs. Bennet showed no notice as she launched into effusive praise of Netherfield, Miss Bingley's gown, and her hosting skills.

Elizabeth cast her gaze about again for Mr. Darcy. Perhaps he was ill?

Elizabeth felt ill.

Miss Bingley said, "Mr. Darcy should be with us shortly." She patted Elizabeth's arm, her smile saccharine. "He had some unexpected business to attend to, but he should be here presently."

Unexpected business? Elizabeth wondered what sort of business could have delayed Mr. Darcy, especially on the day of their engagement party. But Miss Bingley merely continued to talk, guiding them towards the tables as other carriages began to arrive. Jane remained on Mr. Bingley's arm. As they walked, Mr. Bennet asked Mr. Bingley, "How did you and Mr. Darcy meet?"

Mr. Bingley, who had been growing increasingly tense, stammered, "Mr. Darcy and I are friends from school. He always came across so serious, but he has a wicked sense of humor. And he will not abide injustice. The food they served at school was wretched, but most had a stipend from our parents to improve the rations, as they say. A couple of our classmates did not, and Darcy would slip a few quid into their accounts, in secret. He could have used that coin to buy loyalty, but he told no one of his generosity. I only discovered it by accident." Mr. Bingley shook his head, smiling. "He is a good man."

"And it is well of you to speak of him so," Mr. Bennet said.

Elizabeth tried to reconcile the young Mr. Darcy who had given away his own pocket money to help his classmates with the gentleman who had denied Mr. Wickham's inheritance. How could both stories be true?

And how long would this business of Mr. Darcy's take?

Upon setting eyes on the refreshments, Lydia and Kitty forgot decorum and rushed for the cakes and jellies, leaving Elizabeth and Mary behind. Mrs. Bennet, spotting Lady Lucas having just alighted her carriage, abandoned her daughters and rushed towards the family, her arms outstretched, exclaiming, "Lady Lucas, how wonderful to see you."

Lady Lucas, her expression pinched and her fan held rigidly before her, did not extend the same enthusiasm.

Maria Lucas stepped down next, shaking out her skirts before taking the footman's hand to alight. Charlotte followed.

Before the footman could assist, Mr. Collins dashed up, elbowing the footman aside in his haste. "Miss Lucas! Allow me!" he cried at an unnecessary volume.

Charlotte winced but allowed Mr. Collins to take her hand as she descended. She wore a rich wine-red gown that brought out the warm chestnut hues in her eyes.

Mr. Collins beamed. "My dear Miss Lucas, you are a vision! Why, in that dress, your complexion rivals the finest radish from our esteemed Lady Catherine's gardens."

Charlotte stared, nonplussed. "A radish, Mr. Collins?"

"Oh yes!" Oblivious as always, Mr. Collins prattled on. "As plump and wholesome a radish as ever I've seen! You are a feast for the eyes, Miss Lucas!"

Elizabeth pressed her lips together, trying not to laugh. To Elizabeth's surprise, Charlotte gave Mr. Collins a stately nod and smile, responding, "Well, radishes are a fine vegetable. I am glad to bring you joy in that way, Mr. Collins."

"Indeed, indeed!" Mr. Collins replied, puffing out his chest. "You are a generous spirit, Miss Lucas. Come, let us make our way to the tables and partake of the bounty. Lady Catherine has assured me that the fare is exquisite and beautifully prepared, though Mr.

Bingley's cook cannot be as fine as the three Lady Catherine employs at Rosings."

Mr. Collins led her away, chattering loudly about the various vegetables he was partial to and the ways in which radishes were superior to others. Surely even Charlotte's legendary composure had to be tested by such nonsense. But Charlotte merely nodded and smiled, and Elizabeth had the sinking, terrifying feeling that her friend, feeling she had no other prospects, might accept Mr. Collins as a suitor or even a husband.

Elizabeth resolved to talk her friend out of this madness as soon as she could get the lady alone. Unfortunately, if Mr. Collins continued to stick to Charlotte like a fulsome burr, Elizabeth feared she would have little opportunity to make her case this afternoon.

Mary remained by Elizabeth's side as they chatted with other guests, Elizabeth growing more and more concerned as Mr. Darcy remained absent. Mary seemed to have picked up on Elizabeth's distress, her brow furrowed as they moved to a nearby table to sit. "Something is wrong," Mary murmured.

"With Mr. Darcy?"

Mary shrugged, tugging at her sleeves, a nervous gesture Elizabeth had seen her make since childhood. "I do not know. There's something in the air. Like the sensation before a thunderstorm or the way a song can grow discordant, and one knows something is about to change." Mary sighed. "I feel unsettled, and I cannot say why."

"It is not like you to be fanciful, Mary." Elizabeth tried to lighten the mood with a teasing remark, but Mary's frown only deepened.

"Miss Elizabeth?" a soft voice called out.

Elizabeth turned to see a maid waiting, hands clasped anxiously before her. She was a slight thing, with a narrow face and close-set green eyes that peeked out from under her linen cap. Her small nose and thin lips gave her an almost waifish look, accentuated by wispy blonde hair escaping the cap's edges. She stood no taller than five foot two, with a boyish, immature figure swathed in a grey and white striped gown, which, though neatly pressed, hung on her thin frame.

"Yes?" Elizabeth asked.

The maid bobbed a nervous curtsy, eyes downcast. "If you would follow me, miss, sir requests your presence right away," she murmured.

Elizabeth's stomach twisted uneasily. "Mr. Darcy?"

The maid curtsied again, still avoiding eye contact.

Odd of the maid not to refer to Mr. Darcy by name, but she looked young, and a bit overawed by the gathering of gentry around them. Elizabeth glanced at Mary, who merely shrugged and said, "Go on, Lizzy. I shall take care of myself."

Elizabeth nodded and followed the maid, who darted ahead, her steps quick and determined. Elizabeth hastened to keep up, her curiosity burning. Curiosity and an odd tension as Mary's words whispered in the back of her mind, a discordant note that echoed with growing intensity.

CHAPTER TWENTY-TWO

Thankfully, Darcy's valet was still in his rooms when Darcy returned, neck and shoulder dripping with the itching and foul-smelling ink Miss Bingley had struck him with. After scrubbing himself clean, the valet made quick work of changing Darcy's shirt, waistcoat, cravat, and jacket. Still, it had taken too long, and Miss Elizabeth had surely noted his absence and was worried he had abandoned her.

Perhaps he would have done better to wait with ink dripping down his neck and shirt to greet his future fiancée, but pride dictated he present a clean and dignified appearance, especially at his own engagement party. It would be a disaster for the reputation of Miss Elizabeth and her family for her future husband to appear a buffoon, or worse, mad.

Not to mention the stench.

Darcy sprinkled on some extra scent and stormed downstairs, his blood boiling. As with the nonsense of the potion, he had no evidence Miss Bingley had conspired against him to prevent him from meeting Miss Elizabeth upon her arrival at the estate. But the timing was suspicious, and Darcy trusted Miss Bingley as far as he could hurl a pianoforte.

As Darcy reached the front hall, he was startled to see his aunt standing alone near the staircase. Sun slanted through the tall windows, illuminating Lady Catherine's imposing figure. She stood perfectly straight, shoulders flung back haughtily, one hand resting on the polished oak banister. Her expression was resolute, almost severe.

"Aunt Catherine?" Darcy asked in surprise.

At his voice, Lady Catherine turned, the jewels on her fingers flashing in the sunlight. For a brief instant, Darcy thought he saw a calculating gleam in her eye. But then she swayed alarmingly, grasping her cane for balance.

"Fitzwilliam?" she said weakly, lifting a trembling hand to her brow.

A momentary suspicion struck Darcy that his aunt's dramatic reaction was feigned, causing him to hesitate. He quickly chastised himself for such uncharitable doubt. His aunt despised weakness, especially in herself. If she was ill, she would hide it, which explained perfectly why she was here instead of outside with the guests.

Darcy crossed the marble tiles and took her elbow to steady her. "Aunt Catherine, what is wrong?"

Lady Catherine drew herself up. "The heat," she said with a dismissive wave. "It overcame me. But you need not trouble yourself with my affairs. I will be well enough." She swayed again. "Your fiancée awaits, and it is clear you favor Miss Elizabeth Bennet above all things."

Darcy was tempted to take his aunt at her word, again wondering if her behavior was an elaborate ruse. But one could not take risks with a lady of his aunt's years. Darcy sighed, offering her his arm. "Come. We will find a cool place to rest."

"No need," she said, but she took his arm and leaned

on it heavily. They made their slow, painful way to the parlor, where Darcy deposited his aunt in a velvet-cushioned chair. She seated herself almost regally, leaning her cane on the cushion at her side.

Darcy rang for a footman, and after a brief wait, a maid appeared. "Yes, sir?"

He ordered a pitcher of cold water, a glass, and a small towel for his aunt to press against her forehead. The footman inclined his head and disappeared, returning minutes later with the requested items. Darcy dismissed him, poured his aunt a glass of water, and handed it to her. She took a sip, sighing, "This will suffice."

Darcy leaned against a mahogany cabinet, unable to quell his suspicions as he watched his aunt. But she simply pressed the towel to her forehead, her expression passive. Darcy resisted the urge to pace.

"I... regret making you late for this event in your honor," Lady Catherine said, her voice regaining strength. "You should go. Miss Elizabeth will wonder at your absence."

She surely was.

Lady Catherine took another sip of her water. "I worry for you, that is all. You are my nephew, and I want to see you happily settled and secure. Miss Elizabeth may be a beautiful young woman, but her family lacks connections, and you risk your entire legacy on an uncertain prospect." Lady Catherine set down her glass and shifted to face Darcy fully. "I speak as a loving aunt and a concerned relative. Miss Elizabeth may have bewitched you with her charms and her wit, but you must not let it cloud your judgment, Fitzwilliam. I am certain you will see sense, eventually, and realize the folly of choosing such an unsuitable match."

Darcy grit his teeth, struggling to control his temper. "Unsuitable? Aunt, you have done nothing but insinuate Miss Elizabeth's lack of worth, imply she has been deliberately pursuing me for my wealth or status, and spread vicious rumors about her fidelity."

"It is my duty to inform you of potential issues, Fitzwilliam. Your mother and I agreed—"

"My mother is gone." And if his mother still lived, he doubted she would hold him to the dictates of a conversation between her and Lady Catherine when both of their children were infants. "And my decisions are my own to make. Miss Elizabeth may lack in wealth and connections, but she is intelligent and spirited, and we are well-suited. If you are, as you say, feeling better, I will take my leave and rejoin the engagement celebration."

Lady Catherine sighed, as though deeply disappointed. "Very well, Fitzwilliam. I have said my piece." She leaned back in the chair. "I will rest a while longer. If you insist on this foolishness, I can do nothing but be here for you when you see the error of your ways."

Darcy stifled a snort. He had no doubt his aunt would always be there with constant commentary and innuendo, designed to plant seeds of doubt and distrust. But he had no desire to argue further, especially with Miss Elizabeth waiting and worrying.

Bowing, Mr. Darcy took his leave. When he returned to the lawn, the engagement celebration was well underway. Guests chatted in groups, sipping lemonade and punch, and eating the delicacies laid out on the tables. Bingley stood near a shrub of bright pink roses, conversing with Miss Jane Bennet, Miss Bingley and Mrs. Bennet. Bingley caught Darcy's gaze and motioned for Darcy to join them.

Darcy, not wanting to break his promise to his friend to distract Miss Bennet's parents, wended his way through the crowd towards the group while searching for Miss Elizabeth. He spotted Miss Charlotte Lucas and his aunt's odious parson, Mr. Collins, speaking together by one of the tables. Mr. Collins was gesturing animatedly, and Miss Lucas, while polite, clearly struggled to pay attention. Her gaze wandered, and when she caught Darcy watching, she smiled brightly, raising her fingers in greeting.

Miss Elizabeth's three younger sisters were also in attendance. Miss Kitty and Miss Lydia had taken up positions at the dessert table, while Miss Mary, the middle sister, stood to the side, appearing uncomfortable. She scanned the crowd as though searching for someone, her expression anxious. Darcy paused, hesitating. Miss Mary was a quiet young woman, not one to draw attention to herself, but something in her posture, the way her brow furrowed, and her gaze flicked from face to face, made him wonder if she had noticed something amiss.

Worse, he saw no sign of Miss Elizabeth. Where could she be?

To his surprise, Miss Mary, catching his gaze, gave

him a hesitant wave. Darcy nodded and walked towards her, curiosity gnawing at his nerves. Miss Mary had only exchanged the briefest polite words with him since the Netherfield ball, and she never sought his company apart from them.

But if she was waving him over, there must be a reason. And judging by her expression, an upsetting one.

Upon reaching her, he bowed and said, "Miss Mary. How are you enjoying the festivities?"

Miss Mary shrugged. "I am not overly fond of parties. But Elizabeth..." she trailed off, her expression troubled.

"What of Miss Elizabeth?"

Miss Mary fiddled with the sleeves of her gown, twisting the hem between her thumb and forefinger in an obvious nervous gesture. "I do not know. A maid came for her and said 'sir' requested her presence."

"Sir? What sir?"

Miss Mary shook her head. "I assumed it was you."

Darcy's unease grew. "I asked no such thing. Does Miss Elizabeth have any other gentleman callers?"

"No!" Miss Mary's expression grew panicked. "Lizzy would not—she would tell us if—" She stopped abruptly, swallowing hard, and Darcy remembered how young she was.

"I will find her and see what this is about," Darcy said, reassuring her, though his own worry spiked. "Do you know where she went? The maid who spoke to you, did she have a name?"

Mary shook her head, and Darcy ground his jaw, frustrated. It was probably a misunderstanding. Miss Elizabeth should be in no danger here at Netherfield. And if she had other suitors, she would not be foolish enough to engage in an assignation at her own engagement party! Even if Miss Elizabeth was playing Darcy for a fool, she was not a fool herself.

"Do you know which way the maid went?" he asked.

Miss Mary pointed down a path that ran deeper into the gardens, near the pond and thick cluster of trees. "That way. I watched until they were out of sight."

Darcy thanked her, clasping his hands behind his

back to resist the temptation to run off without another word. "I will find your sister and return her safely," Darcy said. And if Miss Elizabeth was engaging in an inappropriate tryst with another gentleman, he would—.

His thoughts skittered to a halt, shame filling him. He would not judge Miss Elizabeth based on his aunt's gossip. Rumors, Darcy was sure, had come straight from Miss Caroline Bingley herself.

Miss Mary wrung her hands, her expression anxious. "Find her, please. I have a terrible feeling, but Lizzy does not listen to me."

Darcy nodded and strode off in the direction Miss Mary had given.

After less than a minute of walking, an unwelcome voice called out from behind him, "Mr. Darcy! Where are you going in such a hurry?"

Darcy turned to see Miss Bingley, her expression eager, her gown a whirl of pale pink silk. She balanced a parasol over her shoulder like a fencing sword.

"Nothing to concern yourself with, Miss Bingley. If you will excuse me."

Miss Bingley hurried after him, ignoring his dismissal. "Are you looking for Miss Elizabeth? I cannot imagine why she would have disappeared. But do not worry, Mr. Darcy, she could not be far. I am sure we will have no problem finding her." Miss Bingley leaned closer, her tone conspiratorial. "Though I hope it is nothing dire. A young woman like Miss Elizabeth, with no fortune or connections, she must be careful about her reputation."

"I doubt any trouble will come to her at Netherfield," Darcy said shortly. He did not like how Miss Bingley was so forcefully working to insert herself into his investigation. "Perhaps it is best you see to our guests."

Miss Bingley frowned. "You seem on edge, Mr. Darcy. Why, just yesterday you seemed content with the match." She gestured to the crowds. "And everyone is having a lovely time."

"You have outdone yourself," Darcy said, hoping flattery would rid him of her attentions.

Miss Bingley beamed. "Then let me assist you in

seeking Miss Elizabeth. It is my duty as a hostess to ensure you have a delightful engagement celebration. And you and Miss Elizabeth will wed soon enough. Why, we shall hold the wedding breakfast at Netherfield. Lady Catherine sent for two of her cooks! Your aunt insisted on it, and..."

Darcy barely heard her, his attention fixed on the path in front of him. He followed it towards the pond Miss Mary had described, noting Miss Bingley's occasional suggestion that they turn right or left, as though she had some deeper understanding of Miss Elizabeth's whereabouts than her claim of ignorance would suggest.

What was Miss Bingley playing at? Was this the cause of his aunt's sudden bout of ill health? If Miss Bingley had dosed Lady Catherine, he would—.

No. More likely, the pair were in it together. Though Lady Catherine might say she was above subterfuge to achieve her ends, her actions suggested otherwise.

But where was Miss Elizabeth?

They rounded a bend, and through the thick branches of a copse of trees, Darcy spotted a figure, and the snatches of Miss Elizabeth's voice, so familiar, filled him with relief, and then fury. "Mr. Wickham, it was not a good idea to come here. I do not think Mr. Darcy would approve—"

Darcy's vision went red as he glimpsed the pair of them standing far too close, his hand on her shoulder in a gesture that bespoke far more than mere acquaintanceship. Mr. Wickham leaned toward her, his mouth moving, but Darcy could not make out their words, not with the rage rushing in his ears.

Whatever Miss Bingley said next, Darcy ignored as he stormed forward, shoving past branches that scraped his skin and tore at his jacket. Mr. Wickham jerked away from Miss Elizabeth, his lips widening into a grin as Darcy approached. "Mr. Darcy. Fancy seeing you here. Shall I offer my congratulations or condolences?"

CHAPTER TWENTY-THREE

The maid led Elizabeth down the garden paths until the sound of the partygoers' conversations faded behind them. Elizabeth's trepidation grew, and she considered turning back, but what trouble could she get into at Netherfield? Besides, she wanted to know what Mr. Darcy needed to discuss away from celebration. Had he learned something new about the love potion or Mr. Beaumont?

They skirted a pond and entered a grove of trees. Elizabeth had to step carefully to avoid the roots that seemed to reach out to trip her. "Where are you taking me?" she asked, glancing around.

The maid gave her a hooded look. "We're nearly there, miss. Just up ahead."

Elizabeth swallowed hard. She wished she had brought Mary along for support. But Mary had been acting strangely, and Elizabeth did not want to burden her with her worries. Not to mention Mary's general disapproval of everything that did not fit her idea of proper behavior.

The maid stopped, and to her shock, Mr. Wickham stepped out from the trees, his fair hair tousled and his smile sharp. "Miss Elizabeth. It's so good to see you."

Elizabeth froze, her heart pounding in her ears. She took a step back. "What are you doing here? I thought—" She glanced at the maid, who dropped into a curtsy, her hands trembling, her gaze downcast.

Mr. Wickham smiled, closing the distance between them, his blue eyes glittering. "A misunderstanding, I'm sure. I assure you, Miss Bingley has given her leave for me to attend, as her guest, of course." Mr. Wickham took Elizabeth's wrist, his warm grip sending a shiver of disgust through her.

"Unhand me," Elizabeth said, yanking her arm away from his grip.

"My apologies," Mr. Wickham said smoothly. He loosened his grip but did not release her. "I did not mean to offend. That is the reason why I asked Miss Bingley to allow you and I to speak alone. I want Mr. Darcy to receive my apology. But I fear he would not hear me out, even after my attempts to express my contrition. With your influence, though, I know he will at least listen to what I have to say."

Elizabeth fought to maintain her composure. If Miss Bingley had contrived not only to invite a gentleman Mr. Darcy despised to their engagement party, and worse, to trick Elizabeth into being alone in his company, no good could come of it. "Mr. Wickham, this is wholly inappropriate. I have no influence over Mr. Darcy, nor does he require my help to hear you out." She turned to the maid. "I think it is time we return to the festivities," Elizabeth said firmly.

The maid, eyes downcast, worried at the fabric of her apron.

Elizabeth frowned. "Please escort me back. Mr. Wickham can find his own way, I am sure."

"Sir. I think—" the maid began, but Mr. Wickham waved her to silence.

"Miss Elizabeth, let us be reasonable." Mr. Wickham rubbed his thumb over the bare skin above Elizabeth's glove. "I hoped we could speak as friends. I have known Mr. Darcy for far longer than you, and I have no wish to make an enemy of him."

"Then you should not have shown yourself here today." The feel of Mr. Wickham's fingers on her skin nauseated Elizabeth, and she twisted away from him.

"I apologize for the deception, Miss Elizabeth," Mr. Wickham said, his tone mild. "And I truly wish to make amends."

"I doubt Mr. Darcy would approve of your behavior." Elizabeth did her best to keep her voice level, knowing she had made a terrible mistake in coming here and hoping that one last attempt to make Mr. Wickham see reason might be enough to get him to release his grip on her, if only for a moment.

But instead of stepping away, Mr. Wickham leaned closer, resting his fingers on her shoulder. "Just a little longer," he whispered, his breath hot against her cheek, "and our show will be complete."

Show? For whom?

Miss Bingley's guests? If Elizabeth were caught here alone with Mr. Wickham with only a maid as chaperone, whatever remained of her reputation and Mr. Darcy's good opinion would be utterly ruined. Elizabeth searched for an escape route, her pulse racing, her muscles tensed for flight. But first, she had to get Mr. Wickham to release his grip.

Elizabeth considered stomping at his feet, but he wore the boots of a soldier, and hers, while stout enough for a country party, would not deter him. Perhaps she could knee him in his bollocks?

From behind her came the snap of a branch and the rustle of leaves, and Elizabeth's heart leapt into her throat. Mr. Wickham turned, and to Elizabeth's horror, Mr. Darcy burst through the trees, his expression furious, his shoulders hunched like a bull. Miss Bingley followed, the ghost of a smile flashing over her features.

Grinning, Mr. Wickham released his grip, a horrid glint to his blue eyes as he said, "Mr. Darcy. Fancy seeing you here. Shall I offer my congratulations or condolences?"

Elizabeth realized she should have kicked Mr. Wickham the moment he grabbed her. Hard. And to the devil with the consequences. But it was too late now.

Miss Bingley gasped, her hand flying to her breast. "Miss Elizabeth! You and Mr. Wickham, alone together? Have you no shame? No regard for Mr. Darcy's feelings?" She turned to Mr. Darcy, her expression contrite. "I am sorry, Mr. Darcy. I never believed the rumors, but now—" She shook her head, fanning herself dramatically. "Oh, Mr. Darcy, I am so ashamed."

Miss Bingley's scheme was plain, and Elizabeth felt sick. How could she have been so naïve as to fall for it? She opened her mouth to defend herself, but Mr. Darcy, his expression murderous, stalked towards Mr. Wickham, his fists clenched. "You have some nerve showing your face here, Wickham," Mr. Darcy snarled.

Mr. Wickham chuckled, stepping back from Elizabeth, his hands up.

"He said he wanted to make amends," Elizabeth tried to explain, even as she recognized herself as totally out maneuvered. "I was lured here."

"Lured here?" Miss Bingley laughed. "Come, Margaret, tell Mr. Darcy what you saw."

The maid opened her mouth and closed it as her green eyes darted between Mr. Darcy, Elizabeth, and Miss Bingley.

Was this the same Margaret who had told Mr. Darcy about Mr. Beaumont? The same Mr. Beaumont who had been proven a fraud? Had Margaret been in on this part of the scheme since the beginning? Elizabeth's chest felt tight, her breaths coming short and fast. Dry leaves crunched underfoot.

A chill ran through Elizabeth as she realized the ruin this painted her in—not just her own reputation destroyed, but her sisters' prospects dashed, most crucially Jane's future with Mr. Bingley. Worse than that, she had also destroyed Mr. Darcy's trust.

Tears stung Elizabeth's eyes. What could she even say to convince Mr. Darcy in the face of all the evidence that she had betrayed him?

"Speak, Margaret, I believe you owe Mr. Darcy an explanation." Miss Bingley's voice rang out like a gunshot in the quiet grove.

Mr. Darcy's face was pale, his voice tightly controlled. "Yes, Margaret. I will reward truthfulness. Tell me what transpired here."

As accusations flew, Mr. Wickham edged backwards, his gaze fixed on Mr. Darcy, but Elizabeth could not concern herself with him now. Not when Elizabeth's future rested on Margaret's words.

Sweat beaded on the maid's sallow brow as she twisted her apron in her bony fingers. Miss Bingley stalked closer, gripping her silk parasol like a club. "Tell him," she hissed, "or I will reconsider your position."

Mr. Darcy, his face pale, spoke with precise syllables. "Yes, Margaret. It is as I said, I will always reward truthfulness. Speak."

Margaret's hands trembled, her bony shoulders hunched inside her oversized gown. "I— MissEliza-bethdidnothingwrong," she blurted out. "Miss Bingley ordered me to bring her here under false pretenses."

Relief rushed over Elizabeth as Mr. Wickham, recognizing the tide had shifted, took another step backwards, spun on his heel, and sprinted away, coat-tails flapping.

"How dare you?" Miss Bingley screamed, her face a rictus of pure fury. " I dismiss you, and forget about a reference. Out of my house and to the devil with you, you conniving—" Dropping the parasol in her rage, she leapt at Margaret, nails bared, fingers curved like claws.

Elizabeth stepped in front of the maid, her hand curling into a fist. When she was a child, and the village boys would tease her younger sisters, Elizabeth had not hesitated to stand up for them, even if it meant a black eye or busted lip. Now, she felt the same rush of anger and power as she planted herself squarely between Miss Bingley and Margaret, drawing her arm back to punch Miss Bingley squarely in the face.

Miss Bingley, unprepared, staggered, raising her hand to her nose. Blood dripped through her fingers.

Elizabeth's fist throbbed, but she could not help the

rush of elation at having finally struck back at the woman who had worked so tirelessly to ruin her reputation. "Keep your threats to yourself, Miss Bingley." Elizabeth's voice was low and deadly. "I have had enough of your bullying. All of your problems are of your own making."

"It was Mr. Beaumont's shoddy work that put us here. If his potion had done as promised, this would be our engagement party," Miss Bingley wheezed. "But I gave Mr. Darcy the antidote, so any pretense of affection between you and Mr. Darcy is gone." She spat a bloody glob onto the roots at Elizabeth's feet. "So have it your way. Marry him. I wish you both the misery you deserve."

"Miss Caroline Bingley," Lady Catherine's voice echoed through the grove.

Elizabeth turned, shocked, to see the imposing woman emerge from the trees, her expression severe, her cane gripped in her white-knuckled hand. "What potion did you give my nephew?"

Miss Bingley's face drained of all color. She glanced wildly from Elizabeth to Mr. Darcy and Margaret. Then, with blood dripping through her fingers, she laughed. "Potion? Nonsense! It is but a jest. You are ill. You ought to be inside, resting, is that not right, Mr. Darcy?" She turned to him, her smile fixed, her eyes frantic.

Mr. Darcy, his arms crossed, said, "It seems my aunt's health has suddenly improved." His tone was wry, and Lady Catherine gave him the briefest nod before turning back to Miss Bingley.

"Indeed." Lady Catherine thumped her cane against the ground as she approached, her back as straight as an iron rod and her expression as unforgiving. "I remember you distinctly telling me your maid would give me upsetting news about my nephew and Miss Elizabeth's courtship. And from what I have overheard, it appears I should be upset."

"It is not what you think—"

"So, you did not conspire to have my nephew compromised through the use of an illicit potion purchased from a peddler named Beaumont?"

"I purchased an antidote, as I said, once I discovered—"

"If there is one thing I despise more than fortune

hunters, Miss Bingley, it is liars." Lady Catherine pounded her cane, her face stormy. "Perhaps Mr. Beaumont will provide information regarding everything he sold you, Miss Bingley. Shall we all visit him together? Margaret?" She turned her gaze on the maid, who shrank into her oversized gown. "Do you know where we might find this Mr. Beaumont?"

Margaret nodded, her wide, green eyes bright with fear. "Yes'm," she said.

"Excellent."

"This is all a misunderstanding," Miss Bingley protested, but her voice was weak, and her shoulders slumped in defeat. "Mr. Beaumont, he tricked me. He said the potion would reveal the potential for love. It would unlock it, and the gentleman I admired would surely be mine. I would have made Mr. Darcy an excellent wife."

"Clearly, you lack the awareness or good breeding to recognize true affection when you see it." Lady Catherine sniffed. "Or you lack the good sense to recognize when you are bested, you silly girl." Turning to Mr. Darcy, she narrowed her eyes. "Now,

Fitzwilliam, are you cured of your misguided affection for Miss Elizabeth Bennet?"

Mr. Darcy furrowed his brow. "Aunt?"

Lady Catherine waved a dismissive hand. "Oh, never mind. Fortunately, none of this nonsense happened in Town. I will see Miss Elizabeth and her sisters are suitably well-dowered to make any gentleman overlook this unfortunate incident. And I must arrange a London season to secure Miss Elizabeth a more suitable match." She peered down her long nose at Darcy. "Unless you insist on clinging to your entanglement?"

Elizabeth's heart sank. She had not thought Lady Catherine's approval mattered to her. But to have her engagement so readily dismissed as only the result of Mr. Beaumont's potion stung. And if Mr. Darcy had received an antidote, it may have changed his feelings. Their engagement, their courtship, the tenderness they had shared might all be a lie, built on a foundation of Mr. Beaumont's potion, Miss Bingley's manipulation, and Mr. Darcy's honor.

Mr. Darcy stood silent, his jaw working, his gaze darting from Margaret to Elizabeth to Miss Bingley and then to Lady Catherine. He raised his chin, his mouth firm, and Elizabeth wondered if he would deny his aunt's assumptions or argue that they were still engaged.

Elizabeth had begun, despite everything, to imagine a lifetime together with this man. But she did not want to trap him into marriage. If he saw no future with her, then she would release him, even if it broke her heart.

"Mr. Darcy," Lady Catherine pressed, "speak up."

"Aunt," Mr. Darcy's voice was tight. "If you could see to Miss Bingley and Margaret, who will soon find employment at Pemberley, I would prefer to speak with Miss Elizabeth about our engagement in private."

CHAPTER TWENTY-FOUR

While his aunt could be overbearing, Darcy was grateful for the alacrity with which she took control of the situation. Miss Bingley and Margaret cowered under Lady Catherine's glare, and within minutes, Miss Elizabeth and Darcy found themselves alone by the pond.

Darcy scrubbed a hand over his face. Miss Elizabeth stood rigidly by his side, her gaze fixed on the water. Darcy ached to pull Elizabeth into his arms, to whisper reassurances, to kiss her fiercely and show her that no love potion could ever compare to the genuine emotion and passion that flowed between them. But did she feel the same affection for him as he felt for her? Or was he foolishly clinging to a fantasy constructed by Mr. Beaumont's potion?

Darcy cleared his throat. "Miss Elizabeth—"

"Mr. Darcy." Miss Elizabeth turned to him, her brown eyes shining with unshed tears. "Your aunt..."

"Lady Catherine is true to her word," Mr. Darcy said, forcing a smile. "She will do her utmost to ensure your sisters are well dowered and provided for, and you..." Darcy trailed off, unable to say the words, the ache in his chest intensifying.

Miss Elizabeth blinked rapidly and stared up at the canopy of bare tree limbs above them, her expression unreadable. "I cannot fault your aunt. If we—" She took a deep, shuddering breath. "If we are not compatible, then it is for the best our engagement ends."

Darcy's heart beat faster. He knew he should agree. They had come together, not through affection, but because a potion had clouded his senses and confused his judgment. But Darcy was not confused now. And he was not under the control of a potion, either. He was in full control of his senses, and he knew his affections for Miss Elizabeth Bennet were genuine.

He only had to find out if she felt the same.

"If we were compatible," he said slowly, "and we married, would you regret that decision?"

Elizabeth took a deep breath, her shoulders trembling. "I would not want to force you into an unwanted union."

"And if the union was not unwanted?" Darcy asked, his heart in his throat. "If the union was desired and eagerly anticipated?"

Elizabeth looked up, her gaze meeting Darcy's, and the air between them grew thick with tension. Darcy's senses heightened with Elizabeth's presence, making him aware of every rustle of dead leaves, every ripple of water over stone, and every movement of her body. He breathed in the sweet scent of her perfume, and as he stepped closer, his fingers brushed hers, and he felt an electric charge race up his arm and settle in his chest.

Darcy watched as her cheeks flushed with color and her eyes widened, as though she, too, sensed the connection between them. "Then I would be thrilled," she whispered. Her fingers curled around Darcy's, and he pulled her to him, wrapping his arms around her slender waist and holding her against his chest.

"I want nothing more than to marry you, Miss Elizabeth," Darcy declared. "My affection for you has grown by leaps and bounds. Whatever Mr. Beaumont's potion may have sparked between us, I cannot credit it for the fire in my soul that burns for you now." Darcy slid his hand up her back and leaned his forehead against hers, her dark curls tickling his skin. "I love you, Miss Elizabeth, with a ferocity that defies description. If you would have me, I will spend the rest of my life proving my devotion to you."

Elizabeth gazed into his eyes, and Darcy caught a glimpse of something in their depths, an emotion that he had only hoped to see returned. "I will gladly have you, Mr. Darcy," she agreed. "My love for you is no potion-induced trick. My heart belongs to you, and it will be yours to cherish forever."

Darcy crushed her against him, breathing in the warm, sweet scent of her skin. He kissed her, her neck, her lips. It was a gentle brush at first, and then more urgent, his desire for her consuming him. Elizabeth's fingers tangled in his hair, and her tongue flicked against his, igniting a fire in his veins. He deepened the kiss, and Elizabeth responded, her soft sighs echoing in his ears.

The world around them faded until it was just the two of them, together, in a cocoon of warmth and passion. He ran his fingers over the curve of her waist, and Elizabeth shivered. Her lips parted as she tilted her head back, her neck exposed for him to trail kisses over her soft skin.

"We should," she giggled, "return to our party. Our guests—"

"Our guests can wait," Darcy said, kissing her throat. "I do not think I can bear to wait the full three weeks for the banns to be read." Or even three minutes. But it would be poor form to ravage his future wife on the grounds of Netherfield, especially with Wickham, the dastardly coward, still running about. So, with an impressive feat of will, Darcy pulled away just enough to keep himself from disgracing the both of them. "My aunt will handle Miss Bingley and Margaret, and I will see to a license, so we can be married next Sunday, no later." He cupped her cheek, his thumb tracing the delicate line of her jaw. "And we have a lifetime of happiness together to look forward to."

Elizabeth grinned, her smile lighting up her face. "Good. Let us not waste another moment." She pulled him towards the path, and Darcy eagerly followed, his hand in hers, his heart light and free, knowing that his love for Elizabeth was true, and her love for him was equally sincere.

CHAPTER TWENTY-FIVE

When Elizabeth and Mr. Darcy returned to the engagement party, still going strong in Netherfield's gardens, Jane and Mr. Bingley stood together, holding hands. Jane's eyes sparkled as she saw her sister, and waving, she called out, "Lizzy, you have been gone for ages. Lady Catherine was about to send out a search party!"

Mr. Bingley gave Mr. Darcy a cheeky wink and added, "Mr. Darcy, Miss Elizabeth, are you enjoying the party? Your sister was worried, seeing as how Caro came back, her nose quite a sight. She said she tripped before she stomped back to the house."

Elizabeth fought a smile, squeezing Mr. Darcy's

hand. "How terrible!" She looked down at her glove, which sported a scattering of dark brown spots where Miss Bingley's blood had dripped. It was ghoulish how pleasing Elizabeth found the evidence of Miss Bingley's injury. But Miss Bingley deserved no less for the pain and trouble she had caused.

"A pity," Mr. Darcy agreed, his tone dry. "But I am sure with proper rest, Miss Bingley will recover."

With Lady Lucas trailing behind, Mrs. Bennet bustled up, her cheeks pink with excitement and relief. "Lizzy, my dear, there you are. You and Mr. Darcy, oh, such a beautiful couple, truly a love match, I dare say. And our Jane and Mr. Bingley—"

"Mama!" Jane interrupted, her face as red as a radish.

"I was simply saying how well you two looked together."

Lady Lucas sniffed, adjusting her lace shawl. "Well, it was certainly a surprise to see Miss Caroline Bingley with such a bruising on her face. Is she truly hurt? We should call for the apothecary, just to be sure."

"She is perfectly fine," Lady Catherine assured her. "I looked over the injury myself, and I am satisfied that Miss Bingley will make a full recovery."

Mrs. Bennet's face was the picture of delight. "How generous of you to worry about her, Lady Catherine. Such a thoughtful soul, you are."

Lady Catherine nodded, accepting the compliment as her due. "My nephew also has news, I am certain." She looked expectantly at Mr. Darcy, who cleared his throat.

"Miss Elizabeth and I have agreed we will wed at the earliest opportunity," Mr. Darcy said, raising Elizabeth's hand to his lips. "We are eager to begin our lives together."

"Ah." Lady Catherine pressed her lips together tightly and then gave Mr. Darcy a curt nod. "I see."

"And would be grateful to have you wish us happy, aunt," Mr. Darcy said, his tone firm.

Lady Catherine smiled thinly. "Of course, nephew. I am overjoyed that you have made such a... surprising choice."

"That is for the best, considering," Lady Lucas agreed, her expression holding the same enjoyment as one who had witnessed a particularly brutal carriage accident. "It would not do for you to have to put off your wedding, Miss Elizabeth. Not after all that scandal."

Lady Catherine lifted her chin. "There was no scandal. Just an unfortunate misunderstanding that was quickly resolved."

"Of course," Lady Lucas said, taking a step back from Lady Catherine's glare. "And my daughter Charlotte also has news. Charlotte!"

Charlotte Lucas, who had been standing with Mr. Collins by the refreshment table, glanced up, her cheeks blooming with color. Elizabeth raised an eyebrow, curious about her friend's sudden discomfort.

Mr. Collins stepped forward, his posture stiff, and announced, "Charlotte and I have reached an understanding."

Elizabeth kicked herself. If only she could have spoken with Charlotte earlier. But then, her friend looked, if not deliriously happy, at least content. She gave Mr. Collins a smile. "Yes. It is true."

Mr. Collins squared his shoulders, puffing up his chest like a bird in mating season. "It is no secret that I have admired Charlotte for some time. She is a lady of both beauty and grace, with excellent connections." He beamed at Lady Lucas and then turned to Charlotte. "I know this may seem sudden, but it is a product of our own deep regard for each other, and I have no doubt our marriage will be a blissful union. As it says in The Book of Common Prayer, 'Love is patient; it is not proud,' and Charlotte is both of these qualities in abundance."

Charlotte stammered something about being overwhelmed and honored by Mr. Collins's attentions. Elizabeth suspected her friend would be anything but blissful in her marriage, but who was she to judge? If marrying Mr. Collins gave Charlotte the stability and security she wanted, Elizabeth could only wish her the best.

"Perhaps, dear cousin, we can have a double wedding," Mr. Collins suggested. "Mr. Darcy and Miss Elizabeth, and then Charlotte and myself. What a glorious day that would be!"

Lady Catherine coughed delicately and muttered, "That will not be necessary, Mr. Collins. There is no need to rush your own nuptials."

Mr. Collins flushed, and his mouth pinched, but before he could respond, Mr. Bingley cleared his throat. "Err..." he said, tugging at his cravat. "Miss Bennet and I also have an announcement to make."

Mrs. Bennet clasped her hands to her bosom. "Jane! How wonderful! I knew you and Mr. Bingley would make a perfect match. Why, I can already envision the wedding breakfast! We must purchase new gowns! And Mr. Bingley will wear his finest breeches! It will be a day to remember for years to come. To think, my two eldest daughters, married in quick succession! Jane, you will be mistress of Netherfield, and Elizabeth—"

"Mama, quiet!" Jane bellowed at a volume Elizabeth had never heard from her sweet and gentle sister. Mrs. Bennet stumbled, her mouth falling open as her daughter added in a more level tone, "Mr. Bingley and I have not made our announcement yet. Please, allow us to speak."

Mrs. Bennet, taken aback, clamped her mouth shut and waved for Jane to continue.

Cheeks pink, Jane glanced at Mr. Bingley, who squeezed her hand. Mr. Bingley said, "I have asked Miss Bennet for her hand in marriage, and she has graciously accepted. Miss Bennet and I have discussed this carefully, and while our engagement may seem hasty, we are confident that we are making the right choice."

"Mr. Bennet!" Mrs. Bennet cried. "It is true! Gloriously true! And exactly as I predicted! Jane and Mr. Bingley are engaged!"

From a neighboring table, where Mr. Bennet and Mr. Hurst were taking slow sips from two glasses that were decidedly not filled with the lemonade and punch that everyone else was drinking, Mr. Bennet said, "I am aware. Mr. Bingley had the courtesy to seek me out before making his happy announcement."

"Did he? And you said nothing to me!" Mrs. Bennet exclaimed. "My nerves! I can hardly handle the shock. How could you be so selfish as to keep such news from me?"

"I offered my blessing." Mr. Bennet shrugged and took another sip of his drink. "Provided Mr. Bingley cares for Jane as she deserves."

"Oh, Jane, forget your father! Both of my eldest daughters will soon wed! What greater happiness could a mother wish for?" Mrs. Bennet's gaze fell on Mary. "Now, Mary, as our next eldest, we must work on your singing! How are you to attract a gentleman accompanying your pianoforte with the reading of scripture and the croaking of a frog?"

Mary's face drained of all color, and Elizabeth felt a flash of sympathy for her younger sister.

"Mama," Elizabeth interrupted. "We have three weddings to celebrate. Let's not overwhelm Mary, Kitty and Lydia just yet."

Lydia, looking for a moment like one who had swallowed a frog, said, "I will be wed before Mary, at least. That is for certain." She tossed her hair, her blonde curls bobbing beneath her bonnet.

Mr. Denny, who was standing nearby, said, "You shall, Miss Lydia." He ducked his head as Mr. Bennet eyed him suspiciously. "If the proper gentleman presents himself," he added, almost mumbling.

Lydia laughed, her high-pitched giggle echoing through the garden. "Of course, for now, we must help with Jane and Lizzy's weddings. And our cousin's. Mr. Collins cannot perform the ceremony on himself, so he must marry here in Hertfordshire." She giggled again. "It will all be so very grand. And Mr. Bingley certainly must hold another ball this spring in celebration."

"Indeed," Mrs. Bennet declared, and as she waxed on about the grandeur of the weddings and balls, Mr. Bingley's complexion took on an oddly greenish tint. Then Jane whispered something in his ear, and Mr. Bingley smiled, squeezing her hand.

The party continued as guests laughed and chatted over lemonade, tea, sandwiches, and tiny iced cakes in the warm autumn sunshine. Even Lady Catherine seemed to enjoy herself. She held court at a table, motioning with her cane she spoke animatedly with Mr. Jones about medicinal herbs while she and Mrs. Bennet compared notes on the virtues of lavender oil.

Elizabeth edged closer to Jane, who sipped lemonade while at the neighboring table, Mr. Bingley suffered the congratulations and marital advice from Mr. Collins. Elizabeth took advantage of the distraction to lean in and whisper, "Whatever did you say to restore our dear Mr. Bingley's good humor?"

"Oh, Lizzy." Jane, eyes sparkling, leaned close and whispered, "I suggested Mr. Bingley and I remove to Derbyshire next year. He found the notion... quite agreeable."

Elizabeth laughed. "I also find the idea of you living near Pemberley most agreeable."

"And as it is written in the Lord's words," Mr. Collins intoned, "'Love is strong as death.' So, it is critical, Mr. Bingley, to ask what flowers your wife would like for the wedding breakfast. Perhaps a bouquet of lilies and roses, to symbolize the enduring love of marriage until one's last rattling breath?"

Mr. Bingley's face took on a decidedly green tinge again. Elizabeth thought Mr. Collins ought to save his flower talk for his own wedding, though Charlotte had perhaps heard enough of it. Or simply agreed to her husband's wishes, not caring deeply for flowers at all beyond a tendency to sneeze when faced with asters in bloom.

As Elizabeth nibbled on her cake, she cast a fond glance at Mr. Darcy, who was chatting with Sir William. He met her gaze and smiled, the expression lighting up his face, and Elizabeth could not help but grin back, feeling a sense of lightness and excitement fill her from the tips of her fingers to the soles of her feet. She could hardly countenance a love potion and scandal had led her to the arms of this gentleman with whom she could share a lifetime of happiness. And perhaps even adventures if the intensity of Mr. Darcy's gaze was any sign.

Jane said, "If marriage agrees with you half as well as betrothal, I suspect you will be blissfully happy, Lizzy. You are positively glowing. And Mr. Darcy is as well."

Elizabeth flushed. "Our mother was right in this, at least. Marriage suits us Bennet sisters quite well. Perhaps I should send Miss Bingley a note of thanks."

Jane laughed. "Judging by the state of your right

glove and Miss Bingley's nose, I think you have expressed your appreciation well enough."

"I suppose." Elizabeth grinned. "Though I hope the blood is not so obvious to our other guests."

Jane nodded, her eyes dancing. "Only to those who know your temper. You must tell me the whole thing when we are home."

Elizabeth took her sister's hand. "And you must tell me how Mr. Bingley finally won your hand and heart."

Jane grinned and squeezed Elizabeth's hand back. "It is not so dramatic a tale as yours, I suspect. But Mr. Bingley, well, he has a way with words and actions. I have no regrets, and I can only look forward to our life together."

"Indeed," Elizabeth said, gazing over at Mr. Darcy who had extricated himself from Sir William and was walking with a determined stride towards her. "I feel the same."

Mr. Darcy joined her and Jane, and as he took her hand in his, Elizabeth leaned against his shoulder and knew whether through magic or chance, her future promised more than merely affection. She had found a love and adventure that outstripped her earlier dreams. And she was ready to embrace it, with Mr. Darcy by her side.

EPILOGUE

Beneath heavy clouds and air sharp with the promise of snow, Miss Caroline Bingley made her furious way towards Mr. Beaumont's wagon. Her nose and eye still throbbed from Miss Elizabeth Bennet's attack, and Caroline's pride stung even worse. No one had ever dared lay hands on her, not her brother Charles and certainly not her nanny or string of governesses, all of whom knew there would be the devil to pay if Caroline told tales to her doting parents. So Caroline did not know how to reconcile Miss Elizabeth's audacity with her own humiliation.

But Caroline had learned one thing from being forced to smile and pretend joy at both Miss Elizabeth and Mr. Darcy's happiness and that of Miss

Bennet and her own brother: Mr. Darcy might have been of no use to her, but love would be. Though Mr. Beaumont's potions had failed her twice, this time, she would force him to deliver love. And if he refused, she would contact the local constable and put the blame for her assault at his feet.

Mr. Beaumont might not have thrown the punch, but the blame was as much his as if he had done the deed himself.

A lantern hung beside the door of the peddler's wagon as she approached, and Caroline could see a shadowy figure stirring within. Mr. Beaumont, no doubt. She knocked with the brass knocker that hung on the door, and a few moments later, it opened, revealing Mr. Beaumont's narrow face.

"Miss Bingley." His voice was flat. "Back again?"

Caroline straightened her shoulders and gave him her most imperious smile. "Indeed. And you will help me this time."

"I hope you are not still set on the same gentleman. Winning his affections, at this point, seems unlikely."

"Forget Mr. Darcy," Caroline wrinkled her nose, the movement throbbing through her face. "I am here for myself."

"One might argue you were always here for yourself," Mr. Beaumont said, his tone amused. He opened the wagon door, waving her inside. "But if you insist, I may have a potion that will give you what you wish."

"Good," Caroline said. She climbed the rickety ladder, her skirts clutched in her hand. Mr. Beaumont's wagon was more cluttered than usual, with dried herbs and plants hanging from the ceiling and bookshelves, and the smell of dust and camphor made Caroline's nose twitch and ache. She paused, her gaze falling on a man seated in a corner, his face half-hidden in shadow.

Caroline narrowed her eyes. She knew that golden hair, that handsome face. "Mr. Wickham?"

George Wickham shifted, his eyes widening. "Miss Bingley? You came alone, I hope?" He glanced towards the wagon's door, clearly frightened.

Caroline lifted her chin. "I do not see how it is your business."

"If you brought Mr. Darcy—"

"Mr. Darcy is too busy with Miss Elizabeth Bennet to bother with the likes of you. Or anyone." Caroline crossed her arms, reminded not only of her failure to secure the gentleman but also, worse, subject to the constant reminders of that failure through wedding talk, wedding planning, and the festive air that filled Netherfield like a particularly obnoxious fog. She turned to Mr. Beaumont, "Enough of Mr. Wickham. Show me what you have for me."

Mr. Beaumont turned to Mr. Wickham. "A few moments, if you would allow. Then we can work on the issue of your transfer."

"Immediate transfer," Mr. Wickham said, slouching in his seat, his expression inscrutable.

Mr. Beaumont led Caroline to his potion cupboard. "Are you certain it is love you seek?" he asked, reaching for a dusty bottle.

Caroline scowled. "What other option do I have? With Mr. Darcy and Miss Elizabeth engaged, I must find happiness elsewhere."

Mr. Beaumont tilted his head, his

dark eyes assessing. "Love and happiness are not necessarily intertwined."

Caroline scoffed. "If my brother and the rest of them are to be trusted, love is the important thing." She rubbed her jaw, her teeth still aching from the memory of Miss Elizabeth's violence. "I deserve to be loved. And I will not be overlooked any longer."

Mr. Beaumont sighed, and after a bit of rummaging, handed her a stoppered vial that glowed with a faint, rose-colored light. "Very well." He gave her a tired smile. "This should do the trick. But I warn you, your love may be closer than you think."

"Excellent," Caroline said, grasping the stopper with her teeth and pulling it off. She tipped the liquid into her mouth, the taste like a mouthful of warm honey, and swallowed. The potion coated her tongue and slid down her throat, its sweetness lingering. The pain in her nose receded as a warm glow spread through her chest. She gave Mr. Beaumont a triumphant look. "I think it is working!"

Mr. Wickham shifted in his seat. Caroline's gaze fell on him, and a rush of longing swept over her. She wanted to be in his arms, to hear his voice murmuring in her ear. She edged closer, and Mr. Wickham glanced up, his blue eyes bright with interest.

A part of Caroline screamed, knowing how ridiculous a life with Mr. Wickham would be, how empty and shallow. But that voice was drowned out by the growing desire, the need to feel Mr. Wickham's warm lips against hers, his hands caressing her bare skin.

"Mr. Wickham?" she breathed, and Caroline took a step towards him. Mr. Wickham sat up straighter, his lips curling into a smile. He patted the bench next to him, and Caroline settled beside him, her pulse racing, her body humming with anticipation.

Mr. Beaumont, his eyes glittering, nodded. "Now, Mr. Wickham, let us address the issue of your immediate transfer. Brighton is quite pleasant, a beautiful place for love to blossom. Do you agree?"

Mr. Wickham took Caroline's hand, sending a shock of energy through her, and Caroline melted against him. "Brighton sounds lovely," Mr. Wickham said, his voice low and husky. "Mr. Beaumont, you have truly outdone yourself."

"I live to serve." Mr. Beaumont sketched a bow and gracefully turned towards his cupboard, offering the couple his back and their privacy as Caroline allowed herself to fall into Mr. Wickham's embrace, her fate sealed.

The End.

I hope you enjoyed reading this book as much as I loved writing it! If so, you can get updates about new releases and specials when you join my email reader club. (Link: https://geni.us/vk-newsletter .) As a welcome, you'll also get an exclusive, free short story from me sent direct to your email :)

Also, if you liked this book, you might enjoy my book, An Unsuitable Governess.

Sparks fly when Miss Elizabeth Bennet takes work as a governess at Pemberley.

Will deceptions, highwaymen, and a rambunctious eleven-year-old girl bring Elizabeth and Mr. Darcy together or tear them apart?

After rejecting Mr. Collins proposal, Miss Elizabeth Bennet assumes the persona of a widow and goes to

Lambton to find work. But when she befriends Mr. Darcy's half-sister Rose and becomes her governess, she must contend with Mr. Darcy, a man she wishes to despise, and Col. Richard Fitzwilliam, a man she wants to love but cannot. With Rose's help, will Elizabeth find the strength to follow her heart?

Mr. Fitzwilliam Darcy would sooner face bandits than return to Pemberley and deal with his stepmother -- alas, he must do both. And when he discovers Miss Elizabeth Bennet in his home, serving as governess to his half-sister Rose, things go from bad to worse. Col. Fitzwilliam is falling for her. Mr. Darcy is too -- or would be, if Miss Elizabeth were at all suitable. Will Mr. Darcy stop denying his heart my before his cousin steals Elizabeth's?

Warning! This book contains: one not at all wicked stepmother, one 100% wicked band of highwaymen, one rambunctious eleven-year-old, one deceptive governess with a heart of gold, one love-stricken colonel, one handsome gentleman in denial of his true feelings, one found treasure, and two happily ever afters to set your heart aflutter.

Here's a short taste of what's inside:

Beneath a gray and weeping sky, a Royal Mail stage-coach trundled north towards Derbyshire. Miss Elizabeth Bennet wished to pretend it was all a grand adventure, but three days being jounced about until her muscles and teeth ached and three nights in tiny coaching inn rooms with the thin, ill-tempered maid Mrs. Gardiner had insisted Elizabeth bring as a chaperone, had robbed Elizabeth of her sense of wonder. Her eyelids were stiff, her hair itched, and she stank.

Across from Elizabeth sat a white-haired, plump woman with spectacles on her nose and a book in her lap. She traced the text with her index finger as she read, pausing occasionally to take a sip from her hip flask or glance out the window at the patchwork fields.

Elizabeth glanced over at her, and then, fearing rudeness, turned her attention back to the pillow on her lap. Gripping the needle between her thumb and forefinger, she sewed. Beside her on the bench, the maid turned chaperone, Adelaide, slept with her head tipped back, mouth parted and snoring like an angry cricket.

"Is it your first time in a public coach?" the woman across from her asked.

Was it so obvious? Elizabeth stabbed the needle into the pillow. "Yes."

"It is not so terrible." The woman closed her book and placed it on the bench beside her. She lifted her hip flask and took a sip. "Have you and your... friend," she glanced at Adelaide. "Come up all the way from London?"

Elizabeth nodded.

"Long journey. You must be exhausted." The woman held out her hip flask. "Have a taste. It will warm your bones."

Elizabeth hesitated. She was not in the habit of accepting refreshments from strangers. "What is it?"

"My special mix for long trips. Go on, then."

Elizabeth glanced over at Adelaide, but the maid did not stir. A fine protector. But Elizabeth was thirsty, and she appreciated the offer of friendship. She took the flask and sipped cautiously.

Liquid fire burned down her throat. Elizabeth coughed, blinking rapidly.

The old woman chuckled. "My specialty. Tea with a touch of lavender and a healthy dollop of gin."

"It is bracing," Elizabeth said, handing the flask back. Now that the initial burn had passed, the drink had warmed her, or at least distracted her from the chill, damp air and Elizabeth's own nerves.

"Are you visiting family up north?"

"In Lambton. And I am hoping to find work as a governess or a lady's companion."

Elizabeth's hands shook. She was really doing this, putting her life and her prospects behind her and seeking work.

After rejecting Mr. Collins' proposal, life at Longbourn had become intolerable. If her aunt and uncle had not visited and yielded to Elizabeth's entreaties to take her with them to Town, she might have buckled, not to Mr. Collins, who had already wed Charlotte, but to another fool with a good income whom Elizabeth did not admire.

No, it was better she left. The life of a governess was

uncertain, and for many unhappy, but if Elizabeth could not marry for love, she would not marry at all. And if she was not to marry, then she needed to provide for herself. She refused to be a burden to her family.

"Lambton! Why, that is my destination. My niece is with child, and I wished to give her some aid, what with her husband being away with Wellington's men. Have you any brothers on the front? We might pray, together."

Elizabeth was touched. "I have no brothers, but if you wish to pray..." Elizabeth had prayed enough this past month for guidance or at least comfort. Perhaps God had guided her here.

"In a bit, perhaps. You are not so fond of embroidery, are you, Miss—?"

Elizabeth bit the inside of her cheek. As tired and sore as she was from the days of travel, once she left this coach, her future became even more uncertain. "Elizabeth," she said.

The maid snorted and rubbed her hand over her cheek. Drool glistened from the corner of her mouth.

"Elizabeth Ben—" No. Once she left this coach, Miss Elizabeth Bennet would disappear. Best to begin now.

"Mrs. Elizabeth Wilson," Elizabeth declared. Wilson was her aunt's maiden name and the one she had chosen to begin her new life.

The old woman's eyebrow twitched. "Mrs. Wilson," she said, smiling with one missing tooth. "Evelyn. Mrs. Evelyn Johnson. It is a pleasure to meet you."

The carriage jerked.

"Huh?" Adelaide rubbed her eyes. The carriage jerked again. Elizabeth gripped the seat as ahead, the driver, astride one of the heavy draft horses, pulled back on the reins, shouting. The horses turned left, slowing beside a carriage which appeared to have tipped onto its side. The horses were gone.

"Goodness! I had not believed the rumors!" Mrs. Johnson exclaimed.

"Rumors?"

"Highwaymen."

Elizabeth swallowed. She peered out the side window. A footman hopped down from the coach. He held a coach gun in hand as he approached the downed carriage.

Adelaide said, "Cor! Mrs. Gardiner said no such thing of us being robbed."

"Perhaps there was an accident," Elizabeth suggested.

"Humph! What accident run off with the horses?"

Adelaide made an excellent point.

The footman returned, shaking his head as he walked back. He spoke briefly to the driver and then walked towards the back of the coach. Elizabeth stood.

"What are you doing?" Adelaide said as Elizabeth opened the stagecoach door.

"Finding out what is going on," Elizabeth said. A cold wind swept into the carriage. "Excuse me," Elizabeth shouted to the footman as he passed. "What happened?"

"Nothing to concern yourself with, Miss."

"Was anyone hurt?"

"No. It is empty."

An empty carriage, no horses, and rumors of high-waymen. Elizabeth shivered.

"We'll be on our way again, Miss, if you would like to get settled in."

Elizabeth thanked him and pulled the door shut.

"Cor," Adelaide said again as the coach rumbled forward. "They gon' report it at the next station?"

"I suppose," Elizabeth said, seating herself again on the bench. As the driver guided the horses, Elizabeth reached up to the shawl around her shoulders and clasped it around her.

Mrs. Johnson took another swig from her flask. "Lambton is a quiet town. You were looking for work as a governess, you said?"

Elizabeth nodded. Thoughts of the empty carriage had driven away fears about her future employment.

"Try the Darcy house," Mrs. Johnson advised, holding the flask out again.

"Darcy?" It could not be the same odious Darcy who had mocked her and then danced with her with all the warmth of a plasterwork. Though Jane, or perhaps their mother, had mentioned Mr. Darcy's estate was in the North.

"At Pemberley. The youngest Darcy girl has been quite the terror since their father's passing, my niece says. She is just eleven and since last summer has driven away three young governesses on her own."

Pemberley. That was the name of Mr. Darcy's estate. Elizabeth had little doubt Mr. Darcy's sister was a terror. She would be following in the family tradition.

"Thank you," Elizabeth said, resolving to find work elsewhere. Highwaymen. Monster children, and now this.

"I would not have suggested it, love, but you were so fierce just then with the footman." Mrs. Johnson held the flask out again, and Elizabeth took it. Mrs. Elizabeth Wilson needed a taste of courage.

Also, you can learn more about **An Unsuitable Governess** and the rest of my books here: https://books2read.com/ap/nO7K17/Violet-King

Lastly, if you enjoyed this book and have a 3-minutes to leave a quick review, I cannot thank you enough! Reviews are how readers decide if they are ready to give a new author a try. For indie authors like me, having readers share their honest views about my books with other readers is a precious gift.

Thank you again so much for reading!

All the best,

Violet

ABOUT THE AUTHOR

Violet King is a Pennsylvania native who loves reading and writing Regency romance. She had some Pride and Prejudice plot bunnies that wouldn't leave her be, so she started writing her first JAFF in 2018. Her first book, Mr. Darcy's Cipher, is inspired by her interest in history and the desire to write about a smart, savvy heroine who saves her country while falling in love.

Violet's other interests include drawing and painting, trying specialty teas (she lived in Japan for a few years and is especially picky about Jasmines and Greens,) cuddling her cats, karaoke, and reading, reading, reading! You can learn more about her books here: https://books2read.com/ap/nO7K17/Violet-King

Made in the USA
Coppell, TX
15 November 2023

24280340R00184